—The—
Queen's
Smuggler

Trailblazer Books

TITLE	HISTORIC CHARACTERS
Attack in the Rye Grass	Marcus & Narcissa Whitman
The Bandit of Ashley Downs	George Müller
The Chimney Sweep's Ransom	John Wesley
Escape from the Slave Traders	David Livingstone
The Hidden Jewel	Amy Carmichael
Imprisoned in the Golden City	Adoniram and Ann Judson
Kidnapped by River Rats	William & Catherine Booth
Listen for the Whippoorwill	Harriet Tubman
The Queen's Smuggler	William Tyndale
Shanghaied to China	Hudson Taylor
Spy for the Night Riders	Doctor Martin Luther
Trial by Poison	Mary Slessor

−The−
Queen's
Smuggler

DAVE & NETA JACKSON

BETHANY HOUSE PUBLISHERS
MINNEAPOLIS, MINNESOTA 55438

Published by Bethany House Publishers
A Ministry of Bethany Fellowship, Inc.
6820 Auto Club Road, Minneapolis, Minnesota 55438

Printed in the United States of America

Library of Congress Cataloging-in-Publication Data

Jackson, Dave and Neta,
  The Queen's smuggler / Dave and Neta Jackson ; illustrated by
Julian Jackson.
    p. cm. — (Trailblazer books)
  Summary: Sarah tries to smuggle a New Testament into England
in order to save the life of William Tyndale, a man imprisoned for
translating the Bible into English.

  [1. Bible—Translating—Fiction.
2. Tyndale, William, d. 1536—Fiction.
3. Great Britain—History—Henry VIII, 1509–1547—Fiction.
4. Smuggling—Fiction. 5. Christian life—Fiction.]
I. Jackson, Neta. II. Jackson, Julian, ill.
III. Title. IV. Series.
PZ7.J132418Qs   1991
[Fic]—dc20   91–4952
ISBN 1–55661–221–4   CIP
                                                AC

The majority of characters in this book were real people. The events involving William Tyndale, King Henry VIII and Anne Boleyn, Sir John and Lady Anne Walsh, John Frith, Thomas Poyntz, Humphrey Monmouth, and Henry Phillips are historical.

However, Sarah Poyntz, the "accident," and Sarah's role in trying to help Tyndale are fictional. Also, Miles' apprenticeship to his relative Thomas Poyntz is conjecture.

DAVE AND NETA JACKSON are a husband/wife writing team who have authored or coauthored many books on marriage and family, the church, and relationships, including *On Fire for Christ: Stories from Martyrs Mirror*, the Pet Parables series, and the Caring Parent series.

They have two children: Julian, an art major and illustrator for the Trailblazer series, and Rachel, a high school student. They make their home in Evanston, Illinois, where they are active members of Reba Place Church.

CONTENTS

Chapter 1

The Letter

SARAH GLANCED AT THE TWO empty places at the end of the large table. Why weren't Papa and Cousin Miles home yet? Their ship was supposed to come in today—Mama had said. The voyage to England and back across the North Sea with merchandise to sell should only take a week at most, unless . . .

"Miss Sarah!" boomed a voice. She looked up startled into the round face of Humphrey Monmouth, one of the English merchants who often stayed at her parents' boarding house here in Antwerp, Belgium. Her face turned red, but he was smiling at her.

"You don't have to worry about your father," Monmouth said, shaking his knife in her direction. "Thomas Poyntz is not only one of the best merchants England has the good fortune to call her own, but a smart seaman as well. He may have waited a day because of weather. Winds are a bit unpredictable in October. Or maybe business took longer than he expected."

"Or delayed by English customs?" suggested Mrs. Poyntz with a slight lift of her eyebrows. Sarah shot

her mother a quick look. Customs? Had the searchers found the books that her father so carefully concealed in the barrels of grain and wine bound for English markets? Although her parents had never spoken of it, her cousin Miles had told her about the bundles of New Testaments Thomas Poyntz regularly smuggled from Belgium into his native England.

"New Testaments in *English!*" sixteen-year-old Miles had said gleefully. "Translated by Master Tyndale himself!"

Sarah had often heard about the man who had once been her cousin's tutor back in England. She was glad when Miles had come to live with them here in Belgium to learn the merchant trade. When he wasn't traveling with her father, Miles often spent time with Sarah, and didn't seem to mind that she was three years younger. But where were her cousin and father now?

"Ah, customs," nodded Humphrey Monmouth. "A minor concern, Mrs. Poyntz. Thomas is a well-respected businessman on both sides of the strait with friends in high places. A minor concern." The stout merchant pushed back his empty plate and beamed at his hostess. "An excellent supper, Mrs. Poyntz! Excellent, indeed."

Just then Sarah heard the front door open and boots stamping. She turned excitedly toward the front hall.

"There, you see?" Monmouth exclaimed. "The seafarers have arrived!"

Sarah didn't wait to be excused from the table but flew into the hall. "Papa!"

Thomas Poyntz wrapped his arms around his only child, then soundly kissed his wife who was close on Sarah's heels. "Sorry we're late, my dear," he said to his wife, shrugging off his cloak. "Business always takes longer than we expect, right Miles?"

Sarah smiled at her cousin who was also taking off his wraps. "Mama told Cook to keep supper hot. And Mr. Monmouth arrived yesterday."

"Humphrey!" Thomas walked with his wife back into the dining room with its wooden beams and inviting table. "Should have known you'd be here warming your britches at my table."

Sarah started to follow her parents, but Miles pulled at her sleeve. "Your father has a letter for you."

"A letter? For me?" Sarah stared at her cousin. "Don't tease me, Miles."

"Honest! And it has the queen's seal on it." With a grin Miles headed for the dining room.

A letter from the queen? Queen Anne? Sarah followed quickly, but Cook was already serving up the empty plates, and everyone was talking at once. She sat at her place and toyed with a half-eaten roll. Finally she could stand it no longer.

"Papa!" she interrupted. "Miles says you have a letter for me."

The voices suddenly were quiet. "Why, yes, I do," said her father, drawing a letter from the leather pouch he wore around his waist. He looked at his wife, then handed the letter to Sarah. "Why don't you read it aloud?"

Sarah turned the folded parchment over. There was a red wax seal, with the queen's crown in the center. Picking up her table knife, she gently loosened the seal and unfolded the page. The letter was dated September, 1534. She looked up at her mother who smiled encouragingly.

The letter was written in a beautiful flowing script, and the first thing Sarah looked for was the signture at the bottom. It said: "Your friend, Anne Boleyn." Sarah's heart was thumping so loudly that she thought others could hear it as she began to read the letter.

My Dear Sarah,

I have often thought of you since our short visit at Little Sodbury Manor a few years ago. You must be a young lady now. And I am now Queen!

Now that you are older, I wonder if you and your parents will reconsider my invitation to come to Court and be one of my maids-in-waiting. There are several other young ladies your age. Please assure your parents that your education in music and literature will continue——I will see to it personally. And of course Court life is an excellent finishing school for young ladies.

I would very much like to see you again, Sarah. After all, you saved my life! But even more than that, you have a refreshing spirit that I value. I am sure we would be good friends. Give my highest regards to your parents. I hope to hear from you soon.

Your friend, Anne Boleyn

Sarah looked up. Mrs. Poyntz was smiling, but her father looked grave.

"How about that, Sarah!" Miles blurted. "A letter from the queen!" Humphrey Monmouth winked at Sarah, but then busied himself filling his pipe.

"Thomas?" Mrs. Poyntz said to her husband. "What do you think?"

Thomas Poyntz frowned. "The same thing I thought three years ago. It is a kind invitation, and I have no disrespect for the queen. She is a dear friend of my cousin, Miles's mother. But I do not want my daughter exposed to all the shenanigans that pass for court life. Look at what happened to Queen Catherine! Look at how Anne herself became Queen!"

"True enough, Thomas!" Humphrey Monmouth lit his pipe, puffed a few times, then exhaled a fragrant cloud of smoke. "But in spite of its weaknesses, an invitation to court is a great opportunity for a young lady. She would meet everyone in English society sooner or later. I have sometimes wondered whether you do your wife and daughter a favor living here in Antwerp away from England for so many years."

Sarah rose, clutching the letter, and slipped out of the room as her father said, "Spoken by anyone else, Humphrey, I might take offense. But I know you are my friend and mean well. It is business only that brings me to Antwerp, and I want my wife and daughter by my side. Sarah is still young. . . ."

The voices in the dining room faded as Sarah ran up the stairs to her bedroom. She shut the door quietly, went over to the window seat and sank onto the cushion. Pressing her cheek against the cool window pane, she looked out into the dark city street. The lamplights were shrouded with an evening fog.

She had often thought of Anne Boleyn—she hadn't been Queen then. But she'd never expected to receive a letter from her! After all, that was three years ago, when Sarah had only been ten years old. . . .

Chapter 2

The Accident

Sarah remembered meeting Anne Boleyn as if it were yesterday.

On one of his business trips to England, Thomas Poyntz had decided to visit his cousin's family in Gloucestershire, a good hundred miles from London. His cousin Lady Anne Walsh and her family lived on a lovely estate in the country.

Thomas Poyntz had taken Sarah along. "Some time at Little Sodbury Manor will do you good," her father said as their rented carriage clipped along past the fields and hedgerows, green with new spring growth. "If you can put up with your two cousins, that is," he teased. "Johnny should be about fourteen now . . . Miles a year younger."

Maybe it was because Mama had decided to stay home in Antwerp and Papa didn't keep reminding her to "act like a lady." Or maybe it was all the room to explore and all the new and wonderful things to do in the country. But Sarah had no trouble "putting up with" her cousins. The boys let her help feed and brush their ponies and taught her how to hold her hand flat while velvety lips nibbled a carrot from her hand. Johnny pointed out the various green shoots sticking up through the dirt in the gardens, naming the flower or vegetable each would be. Miles showed her the tree that had fallen over the creek in the last storm and cheered when Sarah walked across the trunk to the other side. She felt frightened when she looked down at the creek, swollen with spring rains, rushing beneath the tree. But Miles yelled, "Keep your eyes on the other side!" and in no time she was jumping off on the far bank.

Best of all, the boys took her exploring in the woods and meadows and showed her some of their secret places. Sitting under a natural canopy of brambles and vines one day, eating some bread and cheese the boys had smuggled out of the kitchen, Sarah wished she could stay at Little Sodbury forever and ever.

"We better go back," Johnny said, crawling out from under the canopy and standing up. He was nearly as tall as his father. "Mother is expecting company today and wants us home in time to clean up."

"Company?" Sarah asked. She didn't want the Walshes to have company. She wanted her cousins to herself.

"Just a childhood friend of Mother's—Anne Boleyn. She's a lady-in-waiting in the king's court."

Miles snickered. "For *now*. But King Henry has finally divorced his wife, and everybody knows he's got his eye on Anne."

"You shouldn't talk like that about Mother's friend," Johnny scolded. "Come on; we better go back."

But when the three young people walked up the lane toward the house, they saw two fine carriages standing in the drive, the horses still in harness and several servants unloading bags from the boot.

"Uh-oh," said Miles. "She's already here."

Sarah looked at her dirt-smudged hands. She couldn't wipe them on her dress . . . and there were leaves and stickers caught in her petticoat. She brushed at her dress, then tried rubbing her hands with some wet grass. That was a little better—but not much. If Mama were here, she'd be in big trouble.

But the grownups were busy talking and directing the servants where to take the bags. "Ah! Here are the children!" exclaimed Sir John Walsh as they came into the main hall. "Lady Anne, you remember our sons, Johnny and Miles. And this is our niece, Sarah Poyntz."

Two Lady Annes? This was confusing. Her papa's cousin was Lady Anne Walsh, and Anne Boleyn was Lady Anne, too. Then she realized everyone was looking at her, so she dipped her head and tried a curtsy.

"Sarah!" said Anne Boleyn. "You are just what I need in this household of handsome but awkward men. Mrs. Walsh has gone off to oversee dinner preparations, and I need a friend to help me unpack." She smiled and held out her hand.

Sarah looked at the two maids hovering nearby. What did she know about helping a lady unpack?

But she took Anne's hand and went with her to the large guest chamber where numerous gowns were already laid out on the bed. Only after Anne let go of her hand did Sarah remember that her hands were still dirty.

"*And* you have a smudge on your nose," Lady Anne teased, reading her thoughts. The elegant lady nodded toward the hand-painted china basin and pitcher on the washstand. Sarah felt her face go red, but she dutifully poured some cool water into the basin, used some of the lavender soap to scrub her hands and face, then dried them with one of her aunt's embroidered finger towels.

When Sarah was done washing, the maids were already hanging the gowns in the wardrobe. Sarah studied her aunt's guest. Anne Boleyn's dark hair was smoothed back from her face in the English fashion, covered by a pleated headdress rimmed with pearls. The square low neck of her rich red gown was also trimmed with pearls. Small red lips made her dark eyes stand out in the pale, clear face. Anne Boleyn wasn't exactly beautiful, but she was stunning and . . . exciting.

"So. You've cleaned up," said the lady, the same teasing smile playing about her lips. "Now let's go get dirty again."

Sarah looked at her quizzically. "I beg your pardon?"

"Help me choose a good dress for walking. You children have obviously been having a good time. I would love to get away from all the hovering and pampering of these silly servants. Would you take me for a walk and show me some of the sights, Sarah?"

Sarah laughed. "All right, if you'd like."

This is a very curious lady, she thought. Together they chose a simple brown dress with a high neck, with only a touch of lace at the throat and wrists. One of the maids removed Anne's headdress, then caught up the rich dark hair in a net at the nape of her neck.

Sarah's own hair was light brown, with curls and wisps that wouldn't stay tucked under anything. *Oh, to have that rich mane of thick dark hair,* she thought enviously.

Anne sent one of the maids to inform her host and hostess that she and Sarah were going on a walk . . . alone. The two maids protested, but Anne waved them off. "Come along, Sarah. We're a hundred miles from London, and I want some real fresh air!"

At the end of the lane, Sarah held open the gate into the meadow, then latched it behind her new friend. The Walsh boys' two ponies lifted their heads and ambled over curiously.

"Miles is going to teach me to ride!" Sarah said, scratching behind a pony's ears. "Do you know how to ride, Lady Anne?"

Anne Boleyn was feeding a wisp of grass to the other pony. "Yes . . . yes, I learned as a young girl in France."

"Are you French?"

Anne smiled. "No, but I was a maid-in-waiting to Queen Mary when she went to France to marry the French king."

"A *maid*-in-waiting? How old were you?"

"Just twelve. How old are you, Sarah?"

"Ten. How old do you have to be to be a maid-in-waiting?"

"Ten's a bit young," said Anne. "Sometimes I wish . . ." But she fell quiet as they started walking again.

Wish what? Sarah wondered, but did not ask. They walked in silence through the meadow, going through another gate and into the cool woods.

"Would you like to see the tree that fell in the storm? Come on!" Sarah grabbed Lady Anne's hand and skipped along the path. Anne laughed as she trotted to keep up, stopping now and then to unhitch her skirt from a pesky briar.

The massive tree lay on its side across the angry-looking creek. Its bare roots saluted the sky, still draped with clumps of dirt. Most of its branches lay on the other side, though a few trailed their arms and leaves in the rushing water.

"Can we go across?" asked Lady Anne.

"Sure. I walked over once with Miles and Johnny, so I'll go first."

Sarah gathered up her skirt with one hand and reached up with the other to grab a sturdy root. She stepped on the roots and knots which let her scramble to the top side of the fallen tree. "See?"

Reaching down, she helped to pull Anne up the same way she had come. Because she was laughing so hard, Anne had to try two or three times before she stood alongside Sarah.

"I feel ten years old again. If only my maids could see me now!" she grinned. "And what would King Henry say!" Then she really laughed.

Sarah giggled, too. She couldn't imagine Mama or "Auntie Anne," as she called Lady Anne Walsh, walking along a tree trunk. She edged out ahead, keeping her eye on the farthest branch as Johnny had told her. The trunk in the middle was about a man's reach around, and still narrower as it reached the other bank. But then there were branches to hold on to. Sarah had just reached them when a cry cut the still air.

"Sarah! I'm falling!"

Sarah turned around just in time to see Anne Boleyn hit the water, her neat brown dress swirling up around her waist. Anne's head disappeared for a moment under the foamy water, then she appeared gasping.

"Help! Help me! I can't swim!"

Chapter 3

The Visitor

SARAH STARED IN HORROR. Anne Boleyn's arms were flailing helplessly in the stream as her feet tried to find the bottom, only to have the rushing water tumble her against the tree trunk. There was nothing to grasp but the broad trunk which rested nearly six inches above the foaming water.

Without time to think, Sarah scrambled back the way she had come. There, about six feet from Anne, one of the tree's branches was sticking into the water.

"Anne!" she screamed. "Grab the branch!"

But Lady Anne didn't seem to hear. She went under again and reappeared spluttering.

There was only one thing to do. Sarah jumped.

The water was *cold* and rushing faster than it looked. Her clothes felt heavy and seemed to be pulling her down. Shaking the water out of her eyes, Sarah looked frantically for the branch. There it was. She grabbed a handful of leaves, then got a stronger grip with both hands. Now, where was Anne? Sarah looked behind her. Anne was trying to

grasp the tree bark with her fingers, but except for her head and shoulders, the rapid waters seemed to be pulling the rest of her body beneath the tree.

Even without letting go of the branch, Sarah knew Anne was beyond the reach of her arm. But, maybe . . .

"Anne!" she screamed again. "Grab my foot!"

Sarah held on to the branch with both hands, letting her body float toward the frightened lady. Anne grabbed the girl's ankle, and for a moment the extra weight made Sarah think she would lose her grip on the branch. But Anne pulled herself along Sarah's leg until Sarah could reach out a hand. Then Anne also got a grip on the branch, and the two of them huddled in the water holding tightly to the branch and each other.

After a few minutes Anne's white-knuckled grip began to relax slightly. "Sarah, I think I can touch bottom," she said through chattering teeth. Her body sank slightly until her chin rested barely above the water.

Sarah was trying to think what they should do next when they heard, "Hullo! Sarah! Lady Anne!"

That was Johnny's voice!

"Johnny!" Sarah yelled. "We're in the water!"

In a moment Johnny and Miles were scampering along the tree trunk. They paused briefly above the two shivering females, then hurried over to the other bank. Johnny waded in first, pulling himself along by the branches, and grabbed Anne; Miles was right behind and reached out for Sarah.

In a few minutes all four were catching their breath on the bank. "What happened?" Johnny said.

Suddenly Sarah was scared. It was all her fault. She had taken Lady Anne across the fallen tree. Now there she was soaking wet, shivering and muddy. One of the king's ladies-in-waiting! What would Auntie Anne and Uncle John think? What would Papa say? And Anne Boleyn? Was she angry?

To her astonishment Lady Anne began to laugh. She'd lost her hairnet in the water and her dark hair lay plastered to her head and shoulders. The lace at her throat was muddy and limp. But she was laughing.

"Oh, dear children!" she gasped. "If I hadn't been so scared, that would have been the most fun thing that's happened to me in years!"

✧ ✧ ✧ ✧

The foursome made quite a sight as they straggled up the lane to the manor house. But Anne Boleyn simply said she'd foolishly fallen into the stream, and if Sarah hadn't bravely jumped in to help, she would have been in a fine pickle indeed. And wasn't it good of those boys to come looking for them and help them out?

Baths were filled with heated water, muddy clothes rinsed and bundled off to be washed on the morrow, and dry garments provided. Now the three children and their fathers were gathered in the great hall by the stone fireplace waiting for the women to appear for dinner. Sarah thought the crackling warmth of the fire was especially comforting this cool spring evening.

A butler appeared. "Sir John? There is a gentleman at the door. . . ."

"Gentleman nothing," said a voice, and a tall young man dressed in traveling clothes appeared.

"John Frith! My dear young man!" boomed Sir John, and grasped the newcomer by both shoulders. "Come in, come in. We were just about to have our dinner, and you shall join us!"

"I apologize, Sir John, for not informing you of my arrival. There has been some need of secrecy concerning my return to England at this time. . . . Oh, excuse me. I did not realize you had other guests."

"No, no. Come in. You are welcome in our home any time." Sir John turned to Sarah's father. "This is John Frith, a good friend of William Tyndale, of whom I was telling you. John Frith . . . my brother-in-law Thomas Poyntz."

"John Frith!" said Lady Walsh as she came into the hall. "How glad I am to see you! We shall have a magnificent dinner party tonight. And this . . ." she indicated her friend, dressed in a rich blue gown, her damp hair caught once again in the jeweled head-dress, ". . . is an old friend: Lady Anne Boleyn."

John Frith looked a bit startled, but he took each lady's hand with a bow. "I am delighted to meet you, Lady Anne. Am I right that you may soon be our next queen?"

"I see the court gossip spreads far and wide," Lady Anne replied with a small smile.

Sarah blinked. Anne Boleyn to be queen? She had walked a fallen tree trunk with the future queen of England? Sarah tried to catch Miles's eye, but the boys were following the adults to the long table set with fine china, candles, and crystal. When all had taken their places, Sarah was glad Miles was sitting across from her.

When the food had been served and the servants were no longer lifting lids and pouring wine, Sir John beamed at his guests. "Frith, dear fellow, what word do you have of William Tyndale? It has been too long since we have heard any news, and we are eager to know how his translation work goes."

John Frith cleared his throat uneasily. "I should like to share what I know, but, uh, perhaps it is not fitting conversation for this present company." His 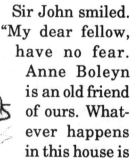 glance rested momentarily on Anne Boleyn, then back to his host.

Sir John smiled. "My dear fellow, have no fear. Anne Boleyn is an old friend of ours. Whatever happens in this house is for our ears alone and will not become gossip for the court. Is that not true, Anne?"

Lady Anne did not seem offended by Frith's discomfort. "I too have heard the Walshes speak of William Tyndale and would like to know more," she said graciously.

Sarah was impatient with this talk. After her dunking, she felt weak with hunger. The juicy lamb on her plate smelled especially good; even the vegetables were swimming in a rich sauce. Miles was attacking his plate with gusto, so Sarah took a big bite of the sweet meat. *Heavenly.*

". . . So you see, dear brother," Sir John was saying to Sarah's father, "we engaged Tyndale as the boys' tutor, and learned much ourselves from his scholarly study of the Scriptures. Whenever we had other guests, he felt compelled to share his desire to translate the Scriptures into our English language. He wants all people—you and me, even these children—to be able to read the Scriptures for themselves in our native tongue, not just hear it read in Latin."

"But surely this was not a popular idea among the clergy," Thomas protested.

"Hardly!" laughed Sir John. "More than one or two left our table with a bellyache—and it wasn't from the food!"

"Yes," said John Frith, "the priests wish to keep the people ignorant so they can continue their wicked and evil practices."

"Father," spoke up Johnny, "remember when the abbot was here and Master Tyndale said, 'If God spares my life, before many years pass I will help the boy that drives the plow to know more of the Scriptures than you do!'"

Sir John laughed even harder. "Oh, yes! The plowboy's challenge!" But then his laughter subsided and he sighed. "Not long after that we realized it was no longer safe for William to remain in England. So he went to Europe to continue his work. We have not seen him since."

"He was a good tutor!" Miles said. "I wish I could see him again."

Lady Anne Walsh turned to John Frith. "But what has happened? Has he been able to print his English Bible?"

"Yes, he has completed the New Testament," nodded the young man, "though not without difficulty. The English authorities have followed him and he has had to move many times. But printed copies of the New Testament are regularly coming into England." A smile tugged at the corners of Frith's mouth. "The bishop has been buying up as many copies as he can lay his hands on and burning them . . . but the money goes straight back to Tyndale to finance his work on the Old Testament!"

Sir John Walsh roared with laughter again, and Anne Boleyn's eyes twinkled. "I would like to meet this Tyndale," she said. "I like his spirit! I myself would like to read the Scriptures in English. It is so tiresome to hear the priests go on and on in Latin, when I understand nothing."

The adults soon retired from the table and continued their conversation around the fireplace in the great hall. Sarah drew Miles aside.

"Is your Master Tyndale in danger?"

"If they catch him," said Miles. "When I was little, Master Tyndale told me about a family who taught their children the Lord's Prayer in English. The priests were so angry that they burned the parents at the stake. They said it was a sacrilege for the common people to speak God's Holy Word in the common language."

Sarah covered her face with her hands. *How horrible.*

"Cousin Sarah," Miles whispered, "I know the Lord's Prayer in English. Both Johnny and I. Our parents taught us."

"But . . . Miles!" Sarah was afraid. "What if the priests find out?"

"Don't worry. My parents are respected by all the nobles and clergy. And we only say it at home when we're alone."

Sarah was silent for a few minutes. Then she said, "Would . . . would you say the Lord's Prayer—in English—for me?"

Miles grinned. "If you wish. Fold your hands; it's a prayer, you know."

With the adults' voices and the crackling of the fire in the background, Sarah folded her hands and closed her eyes while Miles's voice softly chanted the words.

> *Our Father which art in heaven,*
> *Hallowed be Thy name.*
> *Thy kingdom come; Thy will be done*
> *In earth, as it is in heaven.*
> *Give us this day our daily bread,*
> *And forgive us our debts,*
> *As we forgive our debtors.*
> *And lead us not into temptation,*
> *But deliver us from evil.*
> *For Thine is the kingdom, and the power,*
> *And the glory forever. Amen.*

That night, tucked into the trundle bed which pulled out from beneath the big bed her father slept in, Sarah kept saying the words over and over again in her mind. *Our Father which art in heaven . . . Thy kingdom come, Thy will be done . . . Forgive us our debts . . .* As she drifted off to sleep, she thought she had never heard anything as beautiful as the Lord's Prayer.

Chapter 4

In Hiding

SARAH SLEPT LATE the next morning. When she awoke, noises inside and outside the house told her everyone else was up and about. She quickly washed, wiggled into a simple dress and pinafore, brushed her unruly hair as best she could, and stole down the stairs.

There were voices in the great hall and she heard her name. Peering around the great wooden door, Sarah saw her father and Anne Boleyn in earnest conversation.

"Your invitation is very kind, Lady Anne," her father was saying. "But I must firmly decline. Sarah is too young to leave her mother and me...." He held up his hand as he saw Lady Anne about to say something. "And even if she were older, I do not wish my daughter to be exposed to all the stresses and temptations of court life."

"I would take utmost care of her ..." Lady Anne said. Sarah sucked in her breath as she listened.

"Your intentions are no doubt most noble," said Thomas Poyntz. "But your own situation is as yet unclear. Will King Henry be able to marry you as he wishes? He is determined to have a male heir, which the poor queen was unable to give him. But a legal divorce is questionable."

"You don't approve?" Lady Anne's voice was mild.

"That is not the point," said Poyntz. "But I am concerned that my daughter not be caught up in political events beyond even your control."

"Caught'cha eavesdropping," teased a voice in Sarah's ear. Sarah jumped and looked up into the laughing face of John Frith. He took her hand and marched into the great hall.

"It is time for me to leave, Mr. Poyntz, Lady Anne," said the tall young man. "I came to say goodbye."

Poyntz looked relieved to have the conversation interrupted. He shook Frith's hand warmly. The young man had obviously impressed Sarah's father.

Frith then turned to Anne Boleyn.

"My lady, you said you would like to meet Master Tyndale. I don't know whether that will be possible in this life. But you may get to know the man if you read his writings." Sarah saw John Frith draw a slim book from his traveling pouch and place it in Lady Anne's hands. The cover was elegant, decorated with a beautiful script.

"*The Obedience of a Christian Man*," Anne read slowly.

"I wish it were a copy of the New Testament in English," Frith said, "but the latest copies have become ashes in the bishop's bonfires." He smiled wryly.

"But here you have Tyndale's thoughts about the importance of obeying God's Word—which is more important than the traditions of the Church or the decrees of the pope."

Anne laughed. "King Henry would like that! He's not overly fond of the pope's decrees, especially when he wants to divorce a wife." Then, more seriously, "Thank you, John Frith. Your gift will be read and treasured."

A few minutes later the Walsh family joined the goodbyes. As they watched Frith ride out of sight, Sir John Walsh sighed. "I fear for young Frith, as I fear for Master Tyndale. These are intolerant times."

Then abruptly he turned to Sarah's father. "There is a matter I wish to speak to you about, Cousin Thomas. Johnny is, of course, heir to the estate and has taken a keen interest in its management. But Miles," he nodded toward his younger son, "is of a different mind. He has expressed much interest in the merchant trade."

Miles was grinning at Sarah.

"I was wondering," Sir John continued, "if you would be willing to take him as an apprentice for a few years?"

Sarah's eyes widened. She had always wished for an older brother or sister. Was it possible? Would Cousin Miles really come to live with them for a while? Her head was swimming. Overhearing Anne Boleyn's invitation to be her maid-in-waiting . . . her father's refusal . . . all of John Frith's talk about Master Tyndale and people and Bibles getting burned . . .

and now Miles was coming to Antwerp to learn how to be a merchant trader like her father. She felt like she wanted to run away to the special place under the vines in the woods just to think it all over.

As it was, Anne Boleyn would graciously return to the royal court a few days later without Sarah. But when the carriage carrying Thomas Poyntz and his daughter Sarah pulled away from Little Sodbury Manor, Cousin Miles's luggage was stowed in the boot and Miles himself was waving goodbye to his brother Johnny.

❖ ❖ ❖

That had been three years ago.

Now, sitting in the window seat of her bedroom in Antwerp staring at the fog swallowing the street lamps, Sarah remembered how Miles's mother had kissed her son goodbye, then turned to Sarah's father. "Cousin Thomas," she had said, "I know you will take good care of my son. If God gives you opportunity, will you also give a hand to our dear brother in Christ, Master Tyndale, should your paths cross?"

"I will, dear cousin," her father had said. "I am persuaded that his work is a God-given task. I will do what I can."

After one of their trips to England with a shipment of wine and fine silks, Papa and Miles had brought news that King Henry had finally obtained his divorce and married Anne Boleyn. But Sarah assumed she would never hear again from the lady who had fallen in the creek at Little Sodbury.

Now Lady Anne's letter lay in her lap.

Queen Anne's letter.

A light tap at her door interrupted her thoughts. The door cracked open. It was Miles. "Your father sent me to ask you to come down to the parlor."

"Am I in trouble?"

"No, goose," Miles grinned. "But he wants a family meeting about something." His grin faded, replaced by a small frown. "Your father kept disappearing on this last trip to England—even today after we unloaded ship. That's why we were late. But mum was the word to me. Guess we'll find out now."

Tucking the letter under her pillow, Sarah followed Miles to the parlor. Her mother and father were drawn close to the fire, and Humphrey Monmouth sat nearby, puffing on his pipe.

"Come sit down, Sarah . . . Miles," said her father. "There are some matters you must know about." Sarah sat on a footstool by her mother.

Thomas Poyntz took a deep breath. "Both of you, I am sure, remember John Frith, the young friend of William Tyndale—and your own family, Miles—whom we met during our visit to Little Sodbury several years ago. He has been a strong supporter of Tyndale's translation work, traveling between England and Belgium on Tyndale's behalf."

Poyntz paused and looked around at each person. "But I have learned on this recent journey that young Frith has been burned at the stake by Tyndale's adversaries."

"Thomas! No!" cried Mrs. Poyntz.

Miles looked stricken. Sarah buried her face in her mother's shoulder. *Not John Frith! Why? Who could . . . ?*

Then an awful thought crossed her mind. She raised her head and stared wide-eyed at her father. "It wasn't because Queen Anne . . . that book he gave her . . . oh, Papa!"

"No, no, my child," Poyntz assured his daughter. "I am sure Anne Boleyn had nothing to do with it. There are many enemies of the Gospel who desire to keep God's Word out of the hands of the people."

In spite of the horrible news, Sarah felt relieved. Of course Anne Boleyn would never betray a friend. But her father was still talking; she tried to pay attention.

"Not long after we met John Frith at Little Sodbury," he was saying, "Humphrey, here, good fellow, helped me to locate William Tyndale in Germany. He had given Master Tyndale a safe place to stay many years ago in England and has tried to keep track of him since."

Sarah looked at Humphrey Monmouth puffing on his pipe off to the side. What other secrets did the jolly merchant hold?

"Since that time," her father continued, "I have been helping to deliver Master Tyndale's New Testaments to England on our merchant ships—"

"Smuggling, Thomas—call it what it is!" chided Humphrey Monmouth. "This is not the time to shade the truth. Sarah and Miles are not babes."

"Yes, smuggling it is called by those who fear it," Poyntz admitted. "I have not spoken of it much here at home to protect you and Sarah, my dear, though Miles has shared the risk. But with the news of poor Frith's death I have come to a decision."

"Of course," nodded Mrs. Poyntz, relief easing the worry lines in her pale forehead. "It is much too dangerous to ship Tyndale's books at this time. No one will blame you if you stop for a season."

Her husband shook his head. "That is not the decision I have come to. If they have burned John Frith, they will double their efforts to capture William Tyndale. I have decided that he must be given safe refuge—here, with us, at the English Merchants boarding house."

Sarah could hardly believe her ears. She kicked Miles lightly with her toe.

"Oh, Thomas," said her mother.

Thomas Poyntz laid a hand on his wife's arm. "Only if you agree, my dear. There is risk, of course, but we have many friends among the nobility and clergy both in England and also here in Belgium. I would not do this if I did not think the risk worth taking."

Mrs. Poyntz sighed. "You are right, of course, Thomas. But—what of the other merchants who come in and out? Will not the word get around that Master Tyndale is here?"

Humphrey pulled the pipe from his mouth. "Most of our fellow merchants are like me, Mrs. Poyntz—in sympathy with Master Tyndale's desire to place God's Word in the hands of the common plowboy. In my mind there is no safer place for him to be than here."

Thomas Poyntz glanced around at his family. Mrs. Poyntz nodded slowly. Miles was grinning broadly. Sarah smiled and nodded, too.

"Then so be it. Because—uh—he will be here tonight."

"Tonight!" the group chorused as one.

"Yes. In fact . . ." Poyntz raised his hand for quiet. There was a light knock on the front door out in the hall. "That may be our guest now. Miles?"

Miles got up and went to the front door. Sarah jumped up and followed him. Unbolting the door, Miles swung it open.

There, outlined against the fog, a pack on his
back, holding a packet wrapped in oilskin under one
arm and a bag by the other hand, stood a man with a
small beard and kind eyes.

"Master Tyndale!" exclaimed Miles. "It's really
you!"

Chapter 5

The Tutor

AFTER A FEW WEEKS, it seemed to Sarah as if Master Tyndale had been part of the family for a long time. He settled quickly into a spare room on the top floor of the boarding house, his few clothes hung on the wall pegs and his books lined up neatly on the writing table.

The contents of the oilskin packet were laid out on the table along with an inkwell, several quill pens, and a knife to sharpen them. Here Master Tyndale sat, hour after hour, consulting one of his books, then writing on page after page of fresh paper.

He rarely went out, except on Monday afternoons and Saturdays. Sarah didn't know where he went, but when he returned he often looked sad and tired, and the purse that hung from his belt was limp. Mrs. Poyntz was always anxious when he went out and bustled about nervously until he was safely back in the English Merchants boarding house.

Sarah knocked on his door one mid-afternoon in November carrying a tray with a pot of hot tea and some fresh bread from the kitchen.

"Come in."

Sarah pushed open the door and laid down the tray. "You missed the noon meal, Master Tyndale. Mama says you are to stop and eat something."

The lanky man ran a hand through his limp brown hair and smiled wearily. "You are right, Miss Sarah. I get so caught up in my work, I sometimes forget to eat. That bread smells heavenly." He pushed the papers out of the way, broke off a hunk of bread, and poured himself a cup of tea.

Sarah glanced curiously at the many sheets of paper on the table. "What are you doing?"

"Ah!" Tyndale said, swallowing his bite of bread and washing it down with the tea. "I am translating the Psalms from the Hebrew Old Testament into English. Can you read, Sarah?"

"Well, yes," Sarah stammered, "but not very well."

"Try," he urged, handing her the parchment.

Sarah squinted at the words in the tiny script, and began to read.

44

The Lord is my shepherd;
I shall not want.
He maketh me to lie down in green pastures;
He leadeth me beside the still waters.

She looked up. "It's beautiful. But . . . what is it talking about?"

Tyndale raised his shaggy eyebrows. "This Psalm was written by King David, who was a shepherd in his youth. He is praising God that He takes care of us just as a shepherd watches over his sheep."

Sarah laughed. "I like that! Will you teach me some more about what the Bible says?"

Master Tyndale smiled. "It has been a while since I have had a student to tutor—not since I taught Miles and his brother Johnny many years ago at Little Sodbury. Oh, they were little rascals—always playing jokes on me." Master Tyndale chuckled. "I could hardly believe it was Miles when he opened the door the other night. Why, he is practically a grown man!"

Sarah waited impatiently as Tyndale finished his bread and tea. Didn't he hear her question? She watched as he carefully set the dishes back on the little tray.

"Sarah," he said, eyes twinkling as he handed her the tray, "I would be honored to be your teacher—in the Scriptures, English, Latin, history—whatever you want to learn! It would be one way I could repay your parents for their great kindness. But you must ask them for permission."

Thomas Poyntz was delighted with Tyndale's offer to tutor Sarah. Though some girls in England attended private schools, most were taught their letters and the fine arts—painting, needlework—at home. Living in Belgium, Sarah's formal education had been somewhat spotty.

And so the young girl and the scholar began each day that damp winter of 1534 and '35 with two hours of study. When Miles wasn't working with her father, he, too, joined the little class in Tyndale's attic room.

Sarah was fascinated with Tyndale's books. Some were written in Greek and German. And of course there was the big Latin Bible. But her favorite book was the English New Testament.

"Would you show me the Lord's Prayer?" she asked Master Tyndale one day as she and Miles sat on the bench which had been added to the small room for their lessons.

He opened the New Testament to the Gospel of Matthew, the sixth chapter. "There," he pointed, "verse nine."

And there it was: "Our Father which art in heaven, hallowed be Thy name," she read. Beside her, not looking at the page, Miles joined in: "Thy kingdom come, Thy will be done in earth, as it is in heaven . . ."

When they had finished reciting, William Tyndale was smiling. "You know it by heart," he said gently. "That is good, very good. My dear young people, hide

God's Word in your heart where it can never be taken away from you."

Their lesson that day was from Matthew twenty-five. First it was Miles's turn to read, which he did in his deepening man's voice:

"I was hungry and ye gave me meat; I was thirsty, and ye gave me drink; I was a stranger, and ye took me in; naked, and ye clothed me; I was sick, and ye visited me; I was in prison and ye came unto me . . ."

"Who is it talking about?" Sarah interrupted. She knew she asked too many questions, but how else could she understand?

"When the Lord Jesus returns in His glory, this is what He will say to those who will inherit the kingdom of heaven. He is talking to you and me."

"But . . . we never did those things for Jesus. How could we?" Sarah felt dismayed. The Bible was so hard to understand!

"Ah. But read here," Tyndale pointed. So Sarah picked up where Miles had left off.

"Inasmuch as ye have done it unto one of the least of these my brethren, ye have done it unto me."

"Do you see?" said Master Tyndale. "When we feed the hungry and visit the poor souls in prison, it is just as if we are doing it for Jesus himself."

"Then," said Miles thoughtfully, "it is not enough to know what God's Word says, we must *do* as it says."

Master Tyndale smiled broadly. "Exactly." He went over to the window and looked out over Antwerp's rooftops. "There are many poor souls out there who need the love of God," he mused. Then he turned back to Miles and Sarah. "I have an idea. How would the two of you like to go with me next Saturday as part of your lesson?"

"Where?" Sarah felt an odd excitement.

"You'll see. Now," he said, clapping his hands, "that's enough Bible study. Let's talk about geography. We have a whole new world map since Christopher Columbus discovered America in 1492—the same year I was born; that's how I remember it. . . ."

❖ ❖ ❖ ❖

Sarah suspected that Papa had had to overrule Mama's objections to the Saturday outing. But she didn't care. She was just glad to be tramping through the narrow Antwerp streets with Miles and Master Tyndale, tugging her warm cloak tighter against April's chilly air. Belgium's damp winter had not yet given way to the warmth of spring.

"We're heading for the riverfront, aren't we, Master Tyndale?" she guessed after a few twists and turns.

He chuckled. "You're right, Miss Sarah."

Indeed, they were heading for the Schelde River on the north side of Antwerp, the largest and busiest port in Belgium. The river port was only fifty miles from where the Schelde flowed into the sea. To the south of the river's mouth lay the English Channel; to the north was the North Sea.

The trio turned into the narrow street that stretched alongside the docks. The sight of the big three-masted ships straining at their ropes never failed to take Sarah's breath away. Her father's ships—the *Red Queen* and the *Black Princess*—were out on buying trips to Spain, Italy, and northern Africa, and would come back laden with olives, almonds, cheese, grapes, and cut marble.

A tall Englishman wearing a red cloak seemed about to hail them, but Master Tyndale marched steadily past the docks and entered the maze of dense buildings and alleys at the far end. As they passed a baker's shop, he purchased four loaves of bread and gave them to Miles and Sarah to carry.

Two of the loaves were given to a young woman who came to the door of a shabby apartment with three youngsters pulling on her skirt. "Oh, thank'ee, Master Tyndale," she said. "I don't know when me Harry will return from sea. It gets mighty meager when he's away."

Sarah thought she saw the man with the red cloak following behind them. But her attention was distracted by Master Tyndale who was giving the third loaf of bread to an untidy man leaning unsteadily against a building and smelling like liquor. "Get yourself home, my dear man," Tyndale said firmly. "Take this bread to your wife. It may serve to redeem your poor excuses of what has happened to your money."

A short way further, Master Tyndale went down a short flight of steps and knocked on a dingy door. Even though there was no answer, he lifted the latch and pushed the door open. When Sarah's eyes adjusted to the gloom, she saw an old woman hunched in a bed in the corner.

Instantly, Sarah's excitement seemed to drain away.

"Mistress Gilly," Tyndale said cheerfully in Dutch. "You have visitors today." He looked around for a candle, lit it from the not-quite-dead coals in the hearth and soon a soft glow eased the darkness. The old woman smiled wordlessly and clutched Tyndale's sleeve.

Master Tyndale patted the old gnarled hand as he looked around. "Miles," he ordered in a low voice, "build up that fire in the hearth and fetch some water to heat for bathing and tea. Sarah, see if you can sweep up and put some order to the room."

"Can't build a fire without tinder," muttered Miles. But he rummaged some sticks and lumps of coal from the corner, got a blaze going, then disappeared with a pot to find a rain barrel, which the poor often used to collect water.

Sarah found a broom—just old straw that was bound clumsily to a stick—with which she attempted to sweep. In the meantime, Master Tyndale was gently removing the woman's soiled garment and bedding. He rolled the stinking cloths into a bundle, bounded out the door and was back within ten minutes with a fresh bundle.

"See here, Mistress Gilly," he said cheerfully as he rolled the old lady gently from side to side, slipping the clean bedding beneath her, "Mrs. Leerdon did the laundry, just as she promised."

Not for nothing, I'll bet, thought Sarah.

Miles returned with the water and hung the pot over the fire to heat. After a few minutes Master

Tyndale dipped out some of the lukewarm water and gently bathed the old woman's thin body. Miles looked away discreetly, but Sarah helped dry the flabby skin.

Soon the old woman was propped up, wearing a fresh garment, drinking tea, and eating some of the soft bread as best she could with the few teeth she had. As she ate, Tyndale took a Testament from his pouch and read to her, translating into the Dutch language as he went along. Tears glittered in Mrs. Gilly's eyes and the pinched smile never left her face.

"Now, my young friends," said Tyndale, "we must go. But, Mistress Gilly, we will come again." On impulse, Sarah gave the old lady a quick hug. Miles stirred down the fire so it would make good coals, then shut the door behind them.

Sarah pulled her cloak around her once more against the chill as they climbed up the few stairs to the narrow alley. She was still thinking about Mrs. Gilly, and didn't see the stranger who stood in the shadows, not until he spoke.

"William Tyndale, I believe?"

Master Tyndale stopped short and Sarah ran into him. Tyndale half turned and with his arm kept Sarah and Miles behind him. But she peeked under his arm and saw the well-dressed Englishman in the red cloak. He was smiling, but a shiver of fear made her feel cold under her wraps.

Chapter 6

The Stranger

THE NAME IS HENRY PHILLIPS," the man said, lifting his hat in greeting. He was cleanshaven and handsome. "I am a student at the university. I have often heard of your amazing work and have been eager to meet you."

"Yes?" said Tyndale cautiously. "What is it you want?"

"Simply to meet you, and talk. I have long felt frustrated with the Catholic Church, its petty squabbles and meaningless rituals. But until I heard about your ef-

forts to put the Scriptures into the hands of the common people, I felt there was no one I could talk to about the desperate need for reform."

The man fell into step with Tyndale, and Miles and Sarah followed close behind, looking at each other uneasily. They could hear snatches of the conversation, with the man who called himself Henry Phillips doing most of the talking.

". . . was a student at Oxford—yes, your own school . . . unfortunately, I had a quarrel with my father . . . You have heard of Richard Phillips? Yes, he was a member of parliament . . . I decided to pursue a degree in law here in Belgium . . . heard you were in Antwerp . . . am intrigued by the German reformer, Martin Luther, and his ideas of salvation by faith alone and would like to discuss . . ."

The little party had retraced their steps along the riverfront and were turning toward the heart of the city when Tyndale stopped.

"My dear sir," he said to the man in the red cloak, "I am a guest in someone else's house. I would invite you to supper but I cannot presume on my host's hospitality. Perhaps we can meet again."

"By all means," said Henry Phillips graciously. "Ask for me at the Boar's Head Inn. That is where I stay when I am not at the university." He tipped his fine velvet hat to the two young people and walked quickly away.

"Master Tyndale!" said Miles. "I thought for a moment that you were going to walk back to the

English Merchants boarding house with this Mr. Phillips in tow, giving away your hiding place!"

William Tyndale was thoughtful. "It may be as he said—he is sympathetic to my work."

"But no one has introduced him; all we have is his word!"

"I don't like him," Sarah blurted.

"And why is that?" Tyndale teased.

"I don't know. He was following us. I saw him earlier."

"Did you now?"

✧ ✧ ✧ ✧

Everyone talked at once at the supper table. Sarah told her mother about Mrs. Gilly and asked if she could pack a basket with jellies and cakes to take along the next time. Miles told about meeting the man in the red cloak. William Tyndale said Miles and Sarah had made his visits to the poor easier, and seeing the young people had brought a smile to old Mrs. Gilly's face.

"A good lesson in practical Christianity!" said Mr. Poyntz. Then he stroked his short beard thoughtfully. "But I am not sure I trust this Henry Phillips, William."

Tyndale nodded patiently. "We can neither trust him nor mistrust him until we get to know him. If he is seeking God's truth, how can I turn my back on him?"

"Yes-s, but . . ."

"And haven't you said yourself, good Thomas, that the Scriptures in our own language will open the eyes not just of the peasant but the nobleman's son?"

"Well, yes . . ."

"But," Tyndale acknowledged, "it would be best to see for yourself. Will you give me permission to invite Henry Phillips for a meal? Then we can talk together."

The next Saturday Miles was busy helping Mr. Poyntz inventory the new shipments brought by the *Black Princess*. The *Red Queen* was still at sea. But Sarah once again accompanied Master Tyndale as he visited the riverfront slums, this time with a basket of goodies from the Poyntz pantry for old Mrs. Gilly. She also brought some rose-smelling soap, a clean towel, and fresh candles. The old lady was delighted to see her. With great difficulty she half-whispered, half-croaked her name: "Sarah."

On their way home, Tyndale located the Boar's Head Inn and left a message for Henry Phillips to dine with them the following Wednesday if he was in town.

Phillips showed up promptly at five on Wednesday at the English Merchants boarding house with a gift of exquisite Belgian lace for the lady of the house. Mrs. Poyntz was a bit flustered, but accepted the gift and invited Mr. Phillips into the parlor. Sarah hung around but soon grew bored with the conversation and was glad when a servant announced supper.

The table conversation was lively. Phillips showed a keen interest in the merchant business, giving Thomas Poyntz an opportunity to tell about his adventures. "We are planning a trip to the West Indies soon—a whole new market for trade, thanks to that Spanish adventurer, Christopher Columbus."

"I hear you have discovered a market for, well, many new things the English want," said Phillips.

Sarah nearly choked on her meat. Did he mean the New Testaments her father continued to smuggle?

But Thomas Poyntz just chuckled. "Oh, yes, we English seem to want every new thing that can be found."

Phillips entertained them with the latest gossip from London and the king's court. "And the king has a new child—a girl again. Elizabeth they call her."

Sarah's heart seemed to skip a beat. Anne Boleyn had a baby girl? What was she like, this princess? Did she have Anne's rich dark hair and saucy smile?

After supper, Tyndale showed Henry Phillips his translation work on the Old Testament. Phillips admired several books in Tyndale's small library. The talk drifted once again to the "Lutheran reforms" in Germany. . . . Sarah yawned and reluctantly went to bed.

Tyndale seemed to enjoy talking theology with young Phillips. The law student came several times to dinner, meeting some of the merchants who stayed at the boarding house, and quickly engaged them in discussing the need for reform in England.

Everyone seemed to like Henry Phillips—except Sarah. "He's too friendly," she complained to Miles one night after supper, sitting on the stairs while the adults continued their debates around the hearth in the parlor. Even though April's chill had given way to sunny May, evenings still begged for a fire. "He talks to everybody—except us."

"Aw, that's the way university students are," Miles said. "They think they're so important with all their learning. Don't mind Henry Phillips."

Miles wandered off to see if Cook had some leftovers to snitch, but Sarah just sat on the stairs feeling gloomy. She was still sitting in the semi-darkness when the double oak doors leading to the parlor opened and her father came into the hall with Henry Phillips.

"Thank you once again, Mr. Poyntz, for a fine evening," said Phillips, buckling his cape around his shoulders and settling the velvet hat on his head. Then he lowered his voice. "You do know that there is a price on Tyndale's head."

"Yes, I do."

"A man who values money might be tempted to turn him in."

"But God's damnation would rest upon his soul!" said Mr. Poyntz. "Thank you, Henry, for the warning, but we are well aware of the dangers. We will look out for William's safety."

Phillips cleared his throat. "Well! I'm glad of that! It puts my mind at ease. Once again . . . goodnight."

The door closed behind him, and once again Sarah was alone in the shadow of the stairs. Was Henry Phillips warning her father? Or testing him to see if he might be willing to betray Master Tyndale?

✦ ✦ ✦ ✦

Henry Phillips was gone for several days, which was fine with Sarah. She worked hard on her Latin verbs and memorized the Ten Commandments. Pleased with her progress, she went looking for her father who was spending a few days at home before an extended business trip to the south. She found him sitting on the front stoop of the boarding house, enjoying the afternoon sun.

"Papa! Listen to me recite the Ten Commandments!" she coaxed, sitting beside him on the stoop.

"What? And disturb my afternoon nap?" he teased. "Oh, all right, let's hear them."

"Listen, now, Papa, and don't fall asleep. 'I am the Lord thy God . . . thou shalt have no other gods before me. Thou shalt not make unto thee any graven image . . .'"

She was on the ninth commandment, "'Thou shalt not bear false witness against thy neighbor,'" when a shadow fell across father and daughter.

"Excuse me," said the young man who stood with the sun at his back. "I didn't mean to startle you. I am Henry Phillips's servant, and he sent me to inquire if William Tyndale should be in today or tomorrow, as he would like to have lunch with him."

Mr. Poyntz stood. "Yes, I believe he is in. But I hope your master comes today, else I won't get to see him. I am leaving tomorrow on business in southern Belgium and will be gone for several weeks."

"I will tell him!" said the servant. "I am sure he will come as soon as he can."

But Henry Phillips did not arrive that day, and the next morning Thomas Poyntz and Miles left for the city of Barrows. It wasn't until the next day that Sarah answered a knock to find Henry Phillips upon the stoop.

"Good day, Miss Sarah!" said Phillips. "Is Master Tyndale in? I would like to repay his many kindnesses to me by taking him to lunch at the inn."

Sarah left him standing at the door and went running up the stairs to Tyndale's room. When she returned with Master Tyndale close behind, her mother was just inviting Mr. Phillips to stay for lunch.

"I appreciate the invitation, gentle lady," Phillips smiled warmly. "But I am determined to take your house guest to lunch at my expense—though your food would undoubtedly be better than that at the Boar's Head Inn! Ah, Master Tyndale! You are good to interrupt your work for a friend. How about it— will you allow me to take you to lunch? I don't have much time in the city today, but have several matters I would like to discuss with you."

"Why . . . that would be kind of you," Tyndale said. "Mrs. Poyntz? Will it upset your table if I absent myself?"

Mrs. Poyntz shook her head with a gracious smile and went off to supervise the servants in the day's tasks. Phillips and Tyndale took their leave and were disappearing into the first narrow street when Sarah made her decision.

She was going to follow them.

Chapter 7

The Ambush

EVEN THOUGH THE STREETS of Antwerp were narrow and the crowded buildings often kept out the sunshine, Sarah had no need for her cloak. The late May temperature was mild, and at high noon, the sun reached down to warm the cobblestones.

Sarah wasn't sure which way the two men had gone, but she remembered that Phillips had said something about the food at the Boar's Head Inn. She quickly set off for the riverfront along the familiar route Master Tyndale took when they went to see Mrs. Gilly.

As she turned into the first street beyond the boarding house she was rewarded; Phillips and Tyndale were just ahead. There was no hiding; she could only follow undetected if they didn't turn around.

Sarah managed to keep the two men in sight as they turned into first this street, then that. In some places the narrow streets became little more than dark alleys. Phillips and Tyndale turned into one such alley, so narrow that they couldn't walk side by side. Sarah saw Master Tyndale politely motion Phillips to go first, but the younger man insisted that Tyndale go ahead.

When Sarah reached the alley, it took a while for her eyes to adjust to the dark shadows. Up ahead she could see the two men reach the far end which opened up into a wider street. Suddenly she heard Tyndale shout, "Phillips! Run! We have been seized!"

Sarah froze. What was happening? She heard grunts and scuffling. Her heart pounded, and she pressed her back against the alley wall. She half-expected Phillips to come running back toward her, but his tall shape just stood silhouetted in the opening of the alley. Then she heard him say, "This is your man. Take him to Vilvoorde Prison!"

Prison? The word sent a cold shiver down Sarah's back. Her mind was spinning. Tyndale had been captured . . . Phillips had betrayed him!

Then she heard Phillips speak once more. "You, officer. Take two of your men and go to the English Merchants boarding house. Get Tyndale's books and papers."

Sarah didn't wait to hear more. She dashed back down the alley and out into the street. Her feet seemed to fly over the rough cobblestones. Into this street; up that alley. Would she make it in time? She had to get there first!

She rounded the corner of the boarding house just as the pain in her side began to grow intense. But she couldn't stop now. In the door and up the stairs she darted. One flight, two. Up one more to Tyndale's little room.

Bursting through the door, Sarah looked around wildly. Where was the oilskin packet? There, beside the table. She grabbed it up, fat with the pages of Tyndale's translation work. There were more papers on the table but she had no time! From the shelf she grabbed a copy of his English New Testament . . . but where was the copy of the five Old Testament books? Her heart was pounding so loud it sounded like footsteps on the stairs. There—on the stand beside the bed. She snatched it up, and with books and packet clutched to her chest, she flew back down the stairs, ran down the hall to her bed chamber, and slammed the door shut behind her.

She hardly had time to think, yet everything seemed to be happening in slow motion. Throwing back the coverlet of her bed, she arranged the packet and books side by side, smoothed back the cover, then threw herself down upon the bed.

Downstairs she heard pounding on the door and her mother's startled cry. Heavy footsteps ran up the stairs. She heard shouting and furniture crashing. Sarah squeezed her eyes shut: *Oh, God. Oh, Papa.* Then she heard her mother's voice protesting, "What are you doing? What's happening?"

The heavy boots clattered once more down the stairs. One flight, two, three. The door slammed, and all was quiet except for her mother's sobbing.

Sarah got up and opened her door. Her mother was sitting on the stairs crying, and the frightened servants were beginning to come out into the hall to comfort her. "Oh, Sarah!" cried out Mrs. Poyntz. "You're all right! I—I don't know what's happened. Those soldiers went right up to Master Tyndale's room and took all his papers and books. He—he went out with Mr. Phillips, and your father isn't here, and . . ." Her shoulders shook with new sobs.

Sarah went over to her mother, fighting back her own tears. "Mama," she said, sitting down on the stairs and feeling her mother's arms come around her. She had to swallow twice to get the words past the lump in her throat. "Master Tyndale's been captured—taken to Vilvoorde Prison. It was Henry Phillips. Phillips betrayed him!"

Mrs. Poyntz looked at her daughter in shock. "Mr. Phillips betrayed Master Tyndale?"

Sarah nodded, then took her mother's hand and led her to the bed chamber. "But see?" She threw back the coverlet, and there lay the oilskin packet and two bound books.

✧ ✧ ✧ ✧

Thomas Poyntz and Cousin Miles arrived back home as quickly as they could after receiving the urgent message from his wife. Surveying the ransacked room, Mr. Poyntz was furious. "I should never have left! If I ever get my hands on Henry Phillips . . . Tyndale should never have brought that imbecile into this house! He was too trusting."

Miles sat stunned on the little bench in Tyndale's room watching Mr. Poyntz pace back and forth. "How dare the authorities lay a hand on this man!" Sarah's father fumed. "What right did they have? Who was Phillips working for?"

Mrs. Poyntz tried to calm her husband. "Come, Thomas, let's sit down and think what we are to do."

The little family gathered downstairs in the parlor. "Come, Sarah," said her father, "tell me specifically what happened." So once more Sarah told her father and Miles about following Master Tyndale and Henry Phillips as they went off to have lunch, coming to the dark alley, hearing Tyndale's cries and

Phillips' command to take him to Vilvoorde Prison. Then she told of her flight back to the boarding house to rescue his papers and printed Testaments.

Miles looked at her with open admiration in his eyes. "You did a wonderful thing, Sarah," he said.

"I was frightened!"

"Of course you were," Mr. Poyntz said, taking her hands in his. "Anyone would be. The important thing is, you acted when every second counted. I'm proud of you."

Sarah still worried. "But I didn't get the papers on the table. I don't know how much work was lost."

Her father nodded thoughtfully. "Maybe it was just as well. The soldiers think they got something. Maybe they don't know how much they *didn't* get!"

Mr. Poyntz sat quietly for a few minutes, rubbing his beard. "I must get in touch with all the English merchants in the Low Countries to write letters of protest to the government. This is an outrageous breach of our traditional privilege as merchants in a friendly country. And I must try to see William Tyndale at Vilvoorde. . . ." A cloud passed over his face. "What a disgusting, vile castle that is! How could they put such a gentle man in that dungeon?"

✧ ✧ ✧ ✧

Weeks passed, and Thomas Poyntz wrote many letters. He rode the twenty-five miles to Vilvoorde Castle but wasn't permitted to see William Tyndale. Discouraged but determined, he visited all the offi-

cials he could think of who might have influence to release Tyndale. Each effort was rejected. The Emperor of the Low Countries, which included Belgium, was turning against anyone with "reformation" sympathies. England's King Henry VIII, after declaring himself "head of the Church" in order to make his divorce legal, was now trying to prove he was still a "good Catholic." So, the Church's "enemies" were his enemies, too.

May turned into June, but the Poyntz family barely noticed. Fearing that Tyndale's unfinished translation of the Old Testament might never be published, Thomas Poyntz took the oilskin packet Sarah had rescued and disappeared for a few days. When he returned, he no longer had the packet, and all he would say was that he had passed it along to friends for safekeeping.

"The less you know, the safer you are," he said.

"I'm worried about your father," Miles said to Sarah as they sat together on the bench in Tyndale's room, which they often did now. "He is letting his merchant business go; all he does is try to get Master Tyndale released."

"I know." Nothing her father did seemed to work. Even Humphrey Monmouth, the portly merchant who was Thomas Poyntz's closest friend and ally, couldn't cheer him up. Just last night she had heard them talking in the parlor.

"If Tyndale is executed, it will greatly hinder the Gospel," her father told Humphrey. "His scholarship and good name are outstanding! The king never had a more loyal subject, except in one thing—Tyndale believes the Bible must be in the language of the people."

"I agree, dear Thomas," Humphrey had said. "But you are driving yourself beyond reason. You can't tackle the whole British Empire single-handedly. You must give some attention to your work. You have a wife and child to care for."

Her father sighed. "You are right, Humphrey. But there must be *something* we can do—something we have not thought of yet. If only King Henry could read a copy of the English Bible! He might be persuaded it is not 'heresy' but would benefit the people. Then the charges against Tyndale could be dropped."

Now as Sarah sat on the bench with Miles, an idea began to dance about in her mind. When she told her cousin her idea, he looked at her as if she were crazy. "You've got to be out of your mind, Sarah! Only a fool would do such a thing!" Seeing her hurt look, he softened his words. "It's just that . . . it would be dangerous, Sarah."

"But I want to ask Papa anyway. Will you come with me?"

Miles sighed. "If you insist. But I still think it's a crazy idea."

Sarah went to her bed chamber and opened the wooden chest where she kept her treasures. She took out the letter from Queen Anne and Tyndale's copy of the English New Testament. With Miles following, she hunted up her father who was sitting at a writing desk doing accounts. Her mother sat at a nearby window sewing.

Sarah cleared her throat. "Papa, I have something to say." She laid the letter and the New Testament on the writing desk.

"What is this, Sarah?" Thomas Poyntz glanced at the letter. "You know we have refused Anne Boleyn's request."

"I know, Papa. But just listen to me. You have tried everything to get Master Tyndale released. Last night you told Humphrey Monmouth that if King Henry could read a copy of the Bible in English, then he might see for himself that it isn't heretical." Sarah took a deep breath. "If I accepted Queen Anne's invitation to be a maid-in-waiting, I could take this copy of the New Testament and give it to her. *She* would surely show it to King Henry."

Mrs. Poyntz had come to stand beside her husband. A wordless fear was etched in her face.

"No!" said Mr. Poyntz. "I can't let you do that, Sarah. It's too dangerous."

Mrs. Poyntz laid a hand on her husband's arm. When she spoke her voice sounded strange, even faraway. "Thomas, Sarah's right. It's the only way."

Chapter 8

The Storm

THOMAS POYNTZ AND HIS WIFE talked about Sarah's idea for two days. Back and forth they went. But finally they agreed: Sarah could go. When her parents announced their decision, Sarah didn't know if the goose bumps on her arms were excitement or fear.

A letter was sent by messenger to Whitehall Palace in London. One week went by, two . . . But in the third week, a letter returned from Queen Anne. Sarah could come at once.

But there were many things to do to get ready. Who should go with Sarah? Mrs. Poyntz often became ill traveling by sea. Thomas had been cautioned by the other merchants to lie low for a while after his many attempts to speak to the authorities on Tyndale's behalf. It was finally decided that Miles should go with Sarah and accompany her to the palace. Thomas Poyntz informed his captain that the two young people would go on the next scheduled voyage of the *Red Queen*, along with a cargo of olives, wheat, and Belgian lace for the English market.

Mrs. Poyntz hired a seamstress, and the two of them sewed for days so that Sarah could have crisp new undergarments, a traveling outfit, and two new gowns. The traveling dress was a rich green, but simple in style. The other two dresses had the low square neckline common among English ladies, plus a split skirt from waist to hem in front revealing the wonderful embroidery on the underskirt. On one, the sleeves were split in the current fashion to show the puffed undersleeve, gathered with ribbon at several points down the arm. On the other, the sleeve was long and loose, with embroidery all around the wide cuff.

A new cloak and several new caps, including a fashionable "gable" headdress, completed Sarah's new wardrobe. When she tried on the new clothes, Cousin Miles gave a long whistle. "Queen Anne won't even recognize you as the same girl who jumped in the creek after her!"

Miles and Sarah took Mrs. Poyntz to visit Mrs. Gilly. A tear slid down the old lady's face when she heard that Sarah was going away. "I will see to Mrs. Gilly," Sarah's mother said when they got home. "It's one thing I can do to carry on Master Tyndale's work."

"Oh, thank you, Mama," Sarah said, throwing her arms around her mother. She knew it wasn't an easy promise for her mother to make, since Mrs. Poyntz did not feel at home in Antwerp and in the English Merchants boarding house.

There was one last thing that had to be done. Mrs. Poyntz made a pocket on the inside of Sarah's petticoat, where the fullness of the skirt at the hip would hide the bulk of the New Testament Sarah was smuggling into King Henry's court.

✧ ✧ ✧ ✧

The day of the voyage was cloudy and gray. It was high summer, but Belgium's climate was mild and moist. The tide was in and the *Red Queen* rode low in the water as the last of the cargo was stored in her hold. Poyntz had decided that no other New Testaments should be smuggled on this trip; if searchers came aboard they would find nothing and would be more likely to leave Sarah and Miles alone. ·

Cargo ships had only a few cabins—one for the captain and one or two for passengers. The crew bunked wherever they could. Mr. Poyntz brought Sarah's trunk and traveling bag below deck to the tiny cabin reserved for passengers; Miles bunked with the crew.

Mrs. Poyntz set a basket of food on the small table wedged into the cabin. "The crew may be able to eat the ship's fare, but it isn't very appetizing," she whispered in Sarah's ear as she gave her a hug.

"Tide's going out, Uncle Thomas," said Miles, appearing at the cabin door. "Captain says all ashore."

On deck Mr. Poyntz gave Miles last-minute instructions for dispersing the cargo at the London docks. "Cooperate in all ways with the authorities. You don't want any unnecessary attention. But your main responsibility is to get Sarah safely to Whitehall Palace and into the care of Queen Anne. Here is Anne's letter to serve as your introduction."

All too soon the goodbyes had been said and Sarah's parents stood down on the dock. The ropes were cast off, and as the small sails on the bow and at the top of the foremast were loosed, the ship moved out into the Schelde River to ride with the tide. Sarah was on her way to become a maid-in-waiting to Queen Anne of England, and there was no turning back.

❖ ❖ ❖ ❖

The wind was light, and the *Red Queen* moved slowly down the river channel toward the sea. Traveling at five knots, the fifty-mile trip to the mouth of the river took most of the day. The overcast sky was growing dark when the shore shrank back and the river merged with the North Sea.

Sarah and Miles stood near the stern watching the Low Countries retreat behind them. All the sails had been loosed and stood out full from the three tall masts. Sarah shivered and pulled her warm cloak closer about her as the ship leaned with the wind. Her hair was damp from the spraying mist and escaped in moist curls from the cap she wore.

Miles gripped the bulwark. "This is a crazy idea, Sarah," he said, squinting against the wind and

mist. "But I can't bear the thought of Master Tyndale just sitting in that dungeon—or worse. So I'm hoping your crazy idea works."

Sarah had her own doubts. It had seemed like an adventure at first, but as the land disappeared in the fog and darkness, she suddenly wanted to be back home with her mother and father around the parlor fire.

The waves seemed to be getting higher, and Miles and Sarah had to hold tight to the bulwark to keep their balance. Suddenly a voice startled the two cousins. "Miss Sarah!" A ship's crewman was at their side. "A storm is rising fast. The captain says to get below."

Miles helped Sarah down the steps to the lower deck, then went off to see if he was needed to help batten down the ship against the storm. The lantern was swinging from its hook in her cabin and Sarah wondered if she should blow out the candle, but its small light was comforting. She decided against getting into her nightgown and just lay down on her berth. She could feel the hard lump of the New Testament sewn into her clothes and squirmed until she wasn't lying on it.

It had been a long day, and Sarah soon fell asleep to the creak of the ship and the whine of the wind.

❖ ❖ ❖

The next thing she knew, Sarah was flying through the air. Her head knocked against something hard, and it took a minute or two before she realized she'd been thrown out of her berth and had hit her head on the table leg. The cabin was dark; her candle had gone out. The ship was pitching wildly, first to the left, then to the right as if it were hitting the waves broadside. She thought she could hear shouts somewhere, but they were drowned out by the high-pitched howling of the wind and the loud groans of the ship.

Holding on to the table leg, Sarah pulled herself up and crawled back onto her berth. But there was no sleep now. She had to hold on just to keep from being pitched to the floor again. What was happening? Was Miles all right?

Suddenly the small porthole burst open and a rush of water poured into her cabin. Sarah tried to push it closed again, but it was wrenched out of her hands again and again, water pouring in each time. And then abruptly the *Red Queen* turned, lifting Sarah's side of the ship into the air and away from the waves; Sarah slammed the porthole and twisted the latch just seconds before the ship righted itself.

Sarah was soaked; so was her bedding. Holding on to the table, she opened her cabin door and looked out into the passageway. There was no one in sight. Bracing herself, she made her way toward the steps leading to the deck and crawled up toward the hatch.

Sarah lifted her head above the deck. Her heart nearly stopped. A huge wave broke over the bow of the ship, sweeping a sailor off his feet. As she watched in terror, the man slid helplessly toward the side, then was catapulted into the raging darkness.

She opened her mouth to scream, "Man overboard!" but the wave reached the hatch and poured through the opening, knocking her down the steps.

Just then a dark form tumbled through the hatch and nearly fell on top of her. She couldn't see who it was in the dark, but an unfamiliar voice cursed. Then the voice snarled, "Get back in your cabin, girl! Come on!"

"But a man . . ." she spluttered as strong hands pulled her up and roughly pushed her back into her cabin. "A man just fell overboard!" she cried. But the sailor pulled her door shut muttering, "Passengers! Ain't no place for passengers on a cargo ship." A key clicked loudly in the latch.

Sarah lunged back to the door. Locked. *What if . . . what if it was Miles who had been knocked overboard?* She pounded on it with her fists. "Let me out! Let me out!" But the sailor was gone. Frightened, Sarah returned to her berth shivering. Pulling her knees up under her chin, she held on tight to a post. Twice she returned to the door, pounding on it, but it was indeed locked. Finally, back on her berth she laid her head down on her knees and cried. And there she sat throughout the terrible night. Sometimes sleep overtook her, only for her to be jerked awake by the pitching of the ship.

Then someone was shaking her. "Sarah? Sarah, are you all right?"

She opened her eyes and looked into Miles's face.

"Oh, Miles!" she cried, throwing her arms around his neck. "I was afraid you . . . I saw a man go overboard!"

"I know," said Miles soberly. "A new man . . . he didn't answer roll call when the captain took count after the storm."

"The storm is over?" Sarah untangled herself and stretched her cramped legs. Then she realized the sun was streaming in through the little porthole.

Miles laughed ruefully. "Yes, just before dawn. But you look like a bit of wreckage yourself."

With the storm over and Miles safe, Sarah realized she was famished. She dug out Mama's basket of food. The bread was soggy, but the cheese and salted meat were still good. As the cousins sat on the floor of the tiny cabin and ate ravenously, Miles told what had happened during the night. One of the mainsails hung tattered and useless, but the *Red Queen* had hung tight in the storm and none of the cargo had to be dumped.

"But a man was lost," she said slowly. "His poor family." She remembered Master Tyndale bringing bread to the mother in Antwerp with three youngsters hanging on her skirts, waiting for their papa to come home from sea.

"What about the New Testament?" Miles asked. "Is it safe?"

The Testament! Sarah pulled up her skirts until she found the pocket sewn in her petticoat. She pulled out Tyndale's New Testament, slightly damp but otherwise all right. "Oh," she said weakly. "I better wrap it in some oilcloth to keep it dry from now on."

"Just in case you fall overboard, right?" Miles grinned.

The sun was warm and the wind brisk all that day, and the *Red Queen* made good time in spite of the useless sail. They were only five hours behind schedule as they sailed into the mouth of the Thames River that afternoon. Sarah's clothes had dried out, and she had tidied up as best she could. Now she stood on deck watching all the other ships, like a forest of tall masts. As they neared London, she could see the spires of St. Paul's Cathedral thrusting into the sky.

The *Red Queen* finally nosed into the dock near London Bridge in the heart of the city, and for a while there was a flurry of activity as ropes were thrown and dock hands tied her down. Then amid all the hubbub, a shout boomed out.

"Ahoy, Red Queen!"

Sarah saw several soldiers looking up from the dock and shouting.

"No one is to leave the ship! Stand by to be boarded!"

"Uh, oh," muttered Miles in her ear. "King's men. They're going to search for smuggled goods!"

Chapter 9

The Search

Sarah's mouth went dry. She was suddenly very aware of the weight of the small book sewn into her petticoat. What would happen if they found the New Testament she was smuggling into England?

The searchers came aboard, herded both crew and passengers onto the deck and posted a guard while several others went below.

"What is the meaning of this?" demanded the ship's captain. "We are a licensed English merchant ship."

"Who is the owner?" barked one of the soldiers who stayed on deck. He seemed to be in charge.

"Thomas Poyntz, Antwerp, Belgium," Miles spoke up. "I am Miles Walsh, his assistant."

The soldier smirked. "A bit young, aren't you? And who is this?" He jerked a thumb at Sarah.

"This is Miss Sarah Poyntz, daughter of Mr. Poyntz."

"Hmmm." The man looked at Sarah and Miles for a long moment.

"I repeat, what is the meaning of this?" the captain said.

The soldier turned to the captain impatiently. "We have heard on good authority that this ship is smuggling heretical books."

"Preposterous!" said the captain. "I demand—"

"You'll demand nothing! We will see for ourselves whether your 'cargo' matches your shipping list."

Sarah and Miles exchanged glances. On good authority? Did Henry Phillips also betray her father?

Just then the other searchers came back up on deck. "Didn't find a thing," said one.

"Then get this ship unloaded! We'll check the cargo on the dock."

Sarah saw Miles about to speak. The plan had been to hire a carriage and take her to the palace, then return to supervise the unloading of the *Red Queen*'s cargo. But instead Miles said, "Of course. Whatever we can do to assist. You will soon see this is all a mistake."

The searcher ignored him. "You, Captain, take Master Walsh and the young lady here off the ship and wait on the dock. Guard, don't let them out of your sight."

"But what about Miss Sarah's luggage, sir?" the captain protested. "It's still in her cabin."

"No one goes below! We'll see to the bags."

The captain, Miles, and Sarah stood on the dock and watched as the cargo was unloaded. The searchers selected certain crates, barrels, and bundles at random to be opened and the contents searched for smuggled books.

"This is going to take all night," Miles muttered.

Sarah watched the search, a feeling of dread growing in her stomach. If they didn't find the books in the cargo, would she be searched?

Just then the soldier in charge brought her bags. She could tell the contents had been dumped out and then stuffed back in. She blinked back the tears that sprang to her eyes.

"Sir!" said Miles suddenly. "I must beg your leave. Miss Poyntz is on her way to Whitehall Palace at the request of Queen Anne. The queen will be upset if this unnecessary search delays her arrival."

The man hesitated. "A likely story," he growled.

Miles drew Anne Boleyn's letter from his pouch. "Here."

Sarah held her breath while the soldier scowled at the letter in the fading light; dusk was settling over the waterfront. Abruptly he shoved the letter back at Miles.

"She may go."

"I must beg your leave to go with her," said Miles.

"No! Oh . . . all right. But you must return immediately. The *Red Queen*'s cargo is impounded until we clear it."

"Of course," murmured Miles, grabbing Sarah's bags and hustling Sarah off the dock toward the hired cabs.

Not until they were in a carriage heading for Whitehall Palace did Sarah finally relax. And then she began to laugh. "Oh, Miles, you were wonderful!"

"Should have thought of that in the first place," he said.

"I must look a sight!" Sarah groaned. "And all my things are a mess."

The carriage horse clipped along at a good pace, twisting and turning through the narrow streets which followed the Thames River toward the west end of London. Darkness had fallen over the city when the cabby finally reined in his lively horses and called out, "Whitehall Palace."

Miles asked the cab driver to wait, and approached the guards at the walled gate. Sarah craned her neck, staring in fascination at the magnificent house which had once 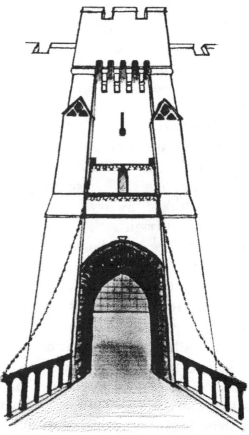 belonged to the Archbishop of York, then the cardinal. The cardinal had fallen out of favor with the king, and the king had taken over the palace for his own use.

"Sarah? Come on!"

With a start Sarah realized the guard had opened the gate and was leading them toward the immense carved doors. They had to show the letter to the guards at two sets of doors before Sarah and Miles were standing in the outer court and a servant was sent to inform the queen.

After about fifteen minutes, the servant returned and motioned Sarah and Miles to follow him. Two more sets of doormen and they were in the inner court. After another wait, a stout gentlewoman swept grandly into the room. "I am Mrs. Stoner, the chaperone for the unmarried maids-in-waiting," the lady said. "The queen is expecting you, Sarah. We thank you, Master Walsh, for escorting your cousin."

Miles looked uneasy.

"I'll be all right, Miles," Sarah said, smiling at him with more confidence than she felt. She laid a hand on his arm. "God be with you."

"And with you," Miles said; his voice sounded strained. He bowed to Mrs. Stoner and turned to go. Then he turned back and drew Sarah aside. "Sarah," he said, "after I get things taken care of at the docks, I am going to visit my parents at Little Sodbury Manor. If you need to contact me in the next few weeks, just send a message. I'll try to see you before I return to Antwerp." He then followed the servant, and the immense doors closed behind them.

"Come now, Sarah," Mrs. Stoner said briskly. "Queen Anne is waiting for you."

Mrs. Stoner led the way up a curving stairway, through several passages and up another stairway. A servant carrying her bags followed. Rich drapes hung at every window; the floors were inlaid marble in wonderful designs. After the first few twists and turns, Sarah realized she could never find her way back the way they'd come. She had never imagined such a big house.

And then Mrs. Stoner stopped before a vaulted door and knocked. A woman servant opened it, and Mrs. Stoner and Sarah entered. Anne Boleyn was sitting on a lounge in a white dressing gown; her long dark hair hanging loose about her shoulders was being brushed by a young woman.

"Sarah! Dear Sarah!" Anne cried, jumping up and coming toward the young girl with her arms outstretched.

Suddenly Sarah felt very strange. The room was very warm; her head felt light. There were bright candles everywhere, yet everything was getting dim. The walls seemed to tip; the floor rushed up at her. Then everything went dark.

Chapter 10

The Maid-in-Waiting

SARAH OPENED HER EYES. Anxious faces stared down at her. Where was she? What happened?

Then she heard a familiar voice. "Sarah? Are you all right? Are you sick?"

Sarah sat up and shook her head, trying to clear the fogginess. Now she remembered. She had come to Whitehall Palace and . . . Oh, no. She must have fainted.

Several pairs of hands helped her up and led her to a lounge chair. Sarah smiled weakly. "I'm really all right. Please forgive me. I—I haven't eaten for several hours and it's been a long journey."

Suddenly she realized with horror that she was in the presence of the Queen of England—and she hadn't even curtsied! She was about to jump up when Queen Anne laid a firm hand on her shoulder. "It's all right, Sarah," the queen said with an amused smile. "You're the first person who's ever fallen at my feet!" And then she laughed that charming laugh Sarah remembered from years before. Mrs. Stoner chuckled, and even the servants smiled.

Anne Boleyn personally escorted Sarah to a small chamber down the passageway from her own rooms. "We can talk tomorrow," she said with her arm around Sarah's waist. "But right now, you need a good night's sleep!" A warm supper was brought; Sarah's clothes were shaken out and hung in the lovely tall wardrobe. A servant brought warm water so she could wash and then she crawled into the big soft bed with curtains draped from the big canopy. As she closed her eyes, Sarah realized that her journey was over . . . but the real adventure had just begun.

❖ ❖ ❖ ❖

The next morning Queen Anne sent for Sarah and they went walking in the private garden behind the palace. Several ladies-in-waiting walked behind at a discreet distance. Sarah told Anne about the storm at sea, her fear that Cousin Miles had been swept overboard, and the searchers ransacking the ship at the London docks looking for "heretical" books.

"But why?" Queen Anne frowned. Sarah hesitated. She knew Anne was a friend, but she didn't know whether she dared say that her father had been smuggling Tyndale's English New Testament into England—at least not yet. But Anne didn't seem to be expecting an answer. "Well! I can see why a young lady might faint dead away after a harrowing night on the sea and soldiers searching through all your luggage. I'm so sorry, Sarah Poyntz! I had no idea—"

They were interrupted by a group of ladies-in-waiting and servants, one of whom was carrying a young child of about two years. Upon seeing Anne, the child held out her arms and crowed, "Mummy!" Queen Anne swooped up the child and said, "Sarah, meet Princess Elizabeth!"

Sarah had almost forgotten that Queen Anne and King Henry had a child! In a moment the princess wiggled out of Anne's arms saying, "Walk!" Elizabeth grasped one of Sarah's fingers as she toddled in the garden path, her nannies and the ladies-in-waiting hovering just behind. Sarah laughed; she had often wished for a little brother or sister.

"I hope you are not too tired," Anne said as they walked with Princess Elizabeth, "because we are having a masquerade tonight! King Henry is quite fond of parties and balls—and especially masks and disguises. Everyone in the palace attends, and many guests. Don't worry, we'll find something for you to wear."

The nannies soon whisked the princess away, and the rest of the day was spent preparing for the masked ball that evening in the Great Hall.

A gown of red and gold appeared in Anne's chamber, along with a Spanish tiara and veil. A servant helped her dress. "You look just like a grand Spanish lady!" the servant said approvingly. "But you need a mask; no one is supposed to know who you are."

The mask appeared mysteriously as well— a glittering red mask which just covered the top half of her face, sweeping out like wings on either side. Sarah joined the other ladies and maids in the Inner Court before going to the Great Hall. There was a "jester" with bells all over her gown, floppy cap, and shoes; an oriental "geisha" with powdered white face; even an "archbishop" in regal robes and towering hat. The other costumes seemed to be a chance to show off elegant gowns, topped with a mask on a stick so it could be held in front of the face.

Sarah gasped in admiration when Queen Anne appeared dressed as a Spanish bride in white gown, white mask and veil. Then it was time to go into the Great Hall. There were a great many lords and ladies, all disguised in strange and wonderful costumes. Sarah was nervous, but felt comforted by Mrs. Stoner's bulky presence at her side.

Musicians were playing but no one was dancing; everyone seemed to be waiting for something. Then there was a commotion by one of the great doors leading into the hall. A hunting horn sounded and a tall, broad man strode into the room followed by several other men. The big man wore green tights, a dark green tunic, a brown jerkin, and a black eye mask, with a pheasant feather in his cap. A quiver of arrows was strapped on his back and he carried a long bow. Several of the other men were dressed in similar fashion, except for one who was dressed as a monk.

A titter ran around the room, then clapping. "Robin Hood and his merry men!" shouted someone, and there was general shouting and laughter. "Hooray for the king!"

The king! Sarah stood on tip-toe trying to see. What a magnificent man. His legs were slender, but his shoulders were so broad he seemed to be two men standing together. He was throwing his head back and laughing with great guffaws, slapping some of the lords on the back and shouting, "Music! Let's dance!"

And then the hall was a swirl of noise and motion as the men and women danced. Sarah wanted to look everywhere at once. The king danced with Queen Anne—"Robin Hood" and the "Spanish bride"—and then they each danced with a dozen others. Two different young men bowed to Mrs. Stoner and requested a dance with Sarah, but the older woman just shook her head and stood protectively at Sarah's side. Sarah felt relieved; she was content tonight to just watch.

The masquerade was still going in full force when Mrs. Stoner escorted Sarah and several of the other young maids-in-waiting back to the private rooms.

Sarah was excited and not sure she could sleep. But a little worry nagged at the back of her mind: Would she ever get any time alone with Anne to give her the New Testament? Would Anne show it to the king?

❖ ❖ ❖ ❖

One week went by, then two. Sarah was kept busy learning the ins and outs of court life. She had music lessons on the lute in the morning, reading lessons in French and Latin in the afternoon, prayers in the chapel, walks in the garden, visits with Princess Elizabeth, dinner parties lasting two or three hours. In between, Sarah was fitted for several new gowns to add to her wardrobe. However, except for the night of the masquerade, she did not see the king.

Sarah was getting anxious. Master Tyndale was sitting in prison; her family was counting on her getting Anne Boleyn's help. Every day she wore the petticoat with the special pocket and the little book. But there were always people around Queen Anne, helping her dress, attending her as she moved about the palace and grounds, serving her at meals. Several times a week the queen met with various lords and ladies and common folks, listening to their requests and pleas. Everyone wanted something from the queen.

Because Sarah could read and write, Anne began to dictate letters for her to write out, which were then sealed with the queen's seal and sent by messenger. At the end of one such writing session, Sarah grew bold. "Your Majesty, could I have a private word with you?"

Anne Boleyn lifted her eyebrows. "Why, yes, Sarah. How about this afternoon when we walk in the garden?"

Before going on her walk, Sarah took the New Testament out of her petticoat pocket and tucked it into the wide sleeve of her gown. And true to her word, Queen Anne asked her ladies-in-waiting and servants to withdraw and she sat with Sarah on a stone bench in the garden. "Did you wish to speak to me, Sarah?"

Sarah took a deep breath. "Do you remember the book that John Frith gave to you at Little Sodbury, the one written by William Tyndale?"

"Yes, of course. *Obedience of a Christian Man*. An excellent book."

"Did . . . did you show it to the king?"

Queen Anne laughed a little. "Oh, yes. He loved Tyndale's attack on the clergy who abuse their privileges. Especially when Tyndale wrote that the king should answer only to God for his actions, not to the pope."

Sarah's heart beat faster. "Then he approves of Tyndale's work?"

Queen Anne shook her head. "Well, not exactly. The king sent for Tyndale to come back to England and be his spokesman, but Tyndale refused. It seems Master Tyndale doesn't want to speak for the king, only for God. But this hurt the king's pride."

Voices could be heard coming toward them in the garden. Sarah didn't have much time. "Your Majesty, Master Tyndale has been put in prison—for printing the Scriptures in English!" She slipped the small book out of her sleeve. "I brought you a gift, a copy of the New Testament that Master Tyndale translated. I—I thought you might show it to the king. If the king likes it, then the charges against Master Tyndale might be dismissed."

Queen Anne looked at the New Testament, then at Sarah, eyes wide. "Tyndale's in prison for printing English Bibles . . . soldiers searched your father's ship, looking for illegal books . . . By God's heaven,

95

Sarah—don't you know you were risking your life to bring me this book?"

It was Sarah's turn to be startled. She hadn't really thought of it as risking her *life*; she had just been afraid the book would be found and taken away. But she had saved the New Testament from Henry Phillips' men; she had survived the storm and made it past the searchers. She couldn't stop now.

"Will you?" she asked again. "Will you read it and see for yourself that Tyndale has done nothing wrong? You're the only one who might influence the king!"

The nannies came into view with Princess Elizabeth. Queen Anne stood up, her face thoughtful. "Put it away, Sarah. But later this evening, bring it to me."

Chapter 11

The King's Gout

SARAH BROUGHT THE NEW TESTAMENT to Queen Anne's private rooms that evening. As she laid it in the queen's hands, she felt a sudden pang of sadness at letting it go. Memories danced in her mind: Master Tyndale helping her read Jesus' words from the Gospels . . . the mad flight ahead of the soldiers in Antwerp to snatch up the Testament from Tyndale's room . . . the weight of the book in her petticoat.

"Thank you, Sarah," Queen Anne said gently, seeing the tears in her eyes. "This is truly a gift."

As she lay in bed that night, Sarah was glad she had memorized several passages from the Testament, "hiding God's Word in your heart," as Master Tyndale had said.

"Our Father," she whispered into the darkness, "Who art in heaven, hallowed be Thy name . . ."

The very next day Anne sent for Sarah. The queen waved her servants out impatiently. When they were alone she exclaimed, "Sarah! I got very little sleep last night for reading your book! How precious to read the Word of God for myself. . . ."

Sarah watched as Queen Anne paced up and down her sitting room, brow furrowed. "To think that Master Tyndale rots in prison for opening up the Scriptures in our own language. . . . You are right, Sarah. The king must see this! It is the greatest gift he could give his people." Anne stopped by a window and stood quietly, thinking.

"But," she finally turned to Sarah, "it will not be easy. King Henry has many moods, and one never knows whether he will be generous and kind, or cranky and unreasonable. Sometimes it depends on whether his gout is causing his foot to pain him!" The queen sighed. "We have been married only two and a half years, and he is not entirely happy with me. You see, he wanted a son, an heir to the throne. . . ."

Unsure whether to respond, Sarah just listened as the queen continued to pace and think out loud. "He gets back from hunting today. . . . He is often tired but satisfied after a hunt. I will arrange a small dinner party for him as a welcome home. It's almost impossible to speak to him alone—all those grooms and gentlemen about. But, we'll just have to try."

Sarah did not see Queen Anne the rest of the day. But Mrs. Stoner brought word that Sarah was to eat with the queen that evening. Sarah's heart seemed to skip a beat. Did that mean eat with the king, too?

Mrs. Stoner brought one of the new gowns which had been made for Sarah—rosy velvet with long flowing sleeves—and helped her dress. She made Sarah practice her curtsy and fussed about royal manners: don't touch the king, don't speak unless spoken to, watch one of the ladies-in-waiting and do as she does. Sarah's hair was brushed back and bound to her head; then a gable headdress was placed carefully over her hair, framing her face.

Mrs. Stoner brought Sarah to Anne's private rooms, then the queen, Sarah, and three other ladies were escorted through a series of wide passageways and down a curving stairway to the king's rooms. The little company paused at a vaulted doorway.

King Henry was sprawled in a large chair, one foot resting on a stool. He was sipping a goblet of wine as several

gentlemen stood about.

Queen Anne swept toward her husband and curtsied. "My lord, I am glad to see that you are safely returned."

"Humph," growled the king. But he took one of Anne's hands and pressed it to his lips. "You are bewitching, as usual, dear wife—and your ladies are charming." He seemed to rise like a tidal wave from the chair, wincing slightly. "Come, come," he said impatiently. "Let's eat."

The king sat at the head of the table with the queen on his right; the ladies and maids-in-waiting were seated to the queen's right, the gentlemen to the king's left.

Sarah suddenly felt homesick. What was she doing here? How she would love to be sitting down to supper with her mother and father and Cousin Miles!

As steaming dishes appeared, Sarah felt overwhelmed by all the food. She ate tiny bites, not knowing how many courses would be served. She lost track after twelve.

The talk bantered about the hunt. Henry had bagged a small boar—not much bigger than a piglet—but the stags had been too swift. "The beasts live free on my own land," he grumbled half in jest. "They should have the decency to stand still long enough for my arrows to find their targets!"

The gentlemen laughed. "Ah, but Your Majesty," said one, "if a beast did not flee, you would probably say it was too lazy to be worth eating."

King Henry chuckled. "No doubt, no doubt." He drained his goblet of wine and shouted, "Cupbearer! More wine! Carver! Another slice of that boar!"

After supper, the king stood and belched. "Ladies, some music. Anything, anything." A servant appeared with several lutes and a flute. Sarah felt alarmed. *Play for the king?* She'd only had two weeks of lessons. But she took one of the stringed instruments and sat with the other ladies and maids-in-waiting around the music stand. Good, the piece was not too hard. One 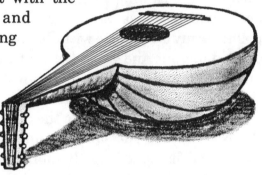 of the ladies began the melody on the flute; the lutes added harmony.

Over the music stand Sarah saw King Henry lean against the tall windows looking out into the twilight, holding his goblet and once again resting one foot on a footstool. Queen Anne went over and sat on the windowsill. Sarah could not hear what the royal couple were saying, but she saw Anne pull the New Testament from a velvet bag, open it and begin reading. Sarah lost her place and frantically searched the music. When she found it again, she glanced up to see the king's face gathered in a deep scowl.

"Enough!" he shouted over the music. The ladies stopped, but he was not looking at them. "Who does this Tyndale think he is! Have I not said we have no need for an English Bible at present? Have I changed my mind?" He kicked over the footstool and stood with his hands on his hips. "Someday! Someday! But it should be done by proper persons—great, learned, Catholic persons! Not some fugitive who ignores my invitations!" He limped toward the door, then suddenly whirled back toward his wife. "And who is polluting my own house with this traitor's nonsense? Get rid of him! And get rid of that book! I'll hear no more!"

The king stormed out, followed by his gentlemen who bowed apologetically to the queen. Still holding the New Testament, Queen Anne gathered up her skirts and hastened up the staircase and through the passages to her own apartments. Sarah and the other ladies followed close behind.

Once in her private chamber, the queen said to the ladies-in-waiting, "Please leave me alone." But in a few moments a servant came to Sarah's room with Anne's request that she return.

Queen Anne came right to the point. "Sarah, it breaks my heart, but . . . you must leave, and as soon as possible. You heard what happened tonight. If King Henry discovers that you are responsible for bringing Tyndale's New Testament into his own palace, you and your family will be in danger. And . . . ," the queen took a deep breath, "there are unfriendly eyes and ears everywhere in this palace. Someone may have seen or overheard us talk about this book—someone who could tell the king."

Sarah was stunned. It was all happening so fast. Couldn't Anne talk to the king again? Was this the end of her hopes? What would happen to Master Tyndale now? She lowered her eyes from Anne's intense gaze and her shoulders sagged.

Then she felt Queen Anne's fingers lift her chin. "Sarah, don't despair," the queen said gently. "I will keep the book and look for another opportunity to plead with the king. But for now, you must go."

Throwing royal manners aside, Sarah threw her arms around Anne's neck. Then she ran from the room, the tears hot on her cheeks.

Chapter 12

The Execution

A MESSAGE WAS PROMPTLY SENT from the palace to Little Sodbury Manor in Gloucestershire county. Miles and his parents came as quickly as they could, but because of the distance it was still several days before the Walsh carriage arrived at Whitehall Palace. Miles asked no questions, but was visibly relieved to walk with Sarah out of the palace gates.

Miles stayed in London to arrange for new cargo to be loaded on the *Red Queen*; Sir John and Lady Anne Walsh took Sarah home with them to Little Sodbury until the ship was ready to sail. It was good to see her cousin Johnny again—almost a grown man and called John now. While waiting to hear from Miles, Sarah walked with John through the woods to the stream which flowed through the manor lands. The old fallen tree still lay across the stream banks. "Strange," she said to John. "This is where everything started."

The Walshes took Sarah to London when Miles sent word that the *Red Queen* was ready to sail. The voyage across the North Sea and down the Schelde

River to Antwerp was uneventful; the breeze was stiff with a tinge of autumn in the air. It had only been a little more than a month since she had left her parents standing on the docks waving goodbye; but so much had happened, it seemed like a year.

As Sarah and her mother unpacked her clothes and hung the new gowns in her wardrobe, Sarah felt older, too. Nothing had changed since she left, and yet . . . everything was different.

Her first evening home, Miles and her parents listened carefully as she told what had happened at Whitehall Palace. When she was done, Mr. Poyntz patted Sarah's hand, but just sat quietly, stroking his beard thoughtfully.

Mrs. Poyntz broke the silence. "Queen Anne did the right thing to send you home. There was nothing more you could do, my child."

"Never did like the idea in the first place," Miles stated. "I'm just glad you're back."

Sarah gave Miles a small smile. But why didn't her father say something? Was he disappointed in her? They had all agreed that taking the English Testament to the king was a good idea. Hadn't her father tried everything else to get Master Tyndale released? But now . . .

Hot tears stung Sarah's eyes. Maybe it had been a foolish idea. Maybe she had just wanted to see Anne Boleyn again, and be her maid-in-waiting. Court life had seemed so exciting. But now the king was even more angry—not just at Master Tyndale, but at Queen Anne, too. Was it her fault? Anne had sent her away. What was going to happen? She didn't know!

Sarah buried her face in her hands. The pent-up feelings of the last few months seemed to roll up from somewhere inside and big gasping sobs shook her body. Then she felt her father's arms around her.

"Sarah, Sarah," he soothed, stroking her hair. "It's all right . . . it's all right. You did what you could; that's all any of us can do. All is in God's hands now."

A year passed. Thomas Poyntz was gone for weeks at a time, still making every effort to get Tyndale released. He left more and more of the decisions regarding buying and selling of goods in Miles's hands, but the business suffered from Thomas's inattention.

With her father and Miles often away, Sarah resumed her weekly visits to old Mrs. Gilly, accompanied by her mother. Mrs. Poyntz seemed to burn with a new passion to visit the poor, lonely souls in the slums who had once been cheered and comforted by Master Tyndale's presence. Mother and daughter baked bread, made soups and jellies, and sewed clothes to give to the needy crowded together in misery down by the docks. The list of those they visited seemed to grow each week. "It is something we can do to carry on Tyndale's work," Mrs. Poyntz often said.

Sarah and her mother were returning home from the docks one day in early August, when they saw two familiar horses tethered outside the English Merchants boarding house. "Thomas!" Mrs. Poyntz cried, bursting into the parlor. "I didn't know you were coming home today!"

Thomas Poyntz hugged his wife and daughter, but Sarah thought he suddenly looked old and tired.

"Thomas?" said her mother. "What's wrong?"

Mr. Poyntz sat down and sighed. "It's Master Tyndale. He has finally had a trial—after fifteen months shivering in that damp dungeon! They have condemned him as a heretic."

"No!" cried Mrs. Poyntz.

Sarah just stared at her father. This wasn't supposed to happen! Queen Anne had said she would talk to King Henry again. As long as there had been no trial, as long as Tyndale was alive, they had hoped.

"When?" asked her mother.

Mr. Poyntz ran his hands through his hair. "I'm not sure, but we must find out. Miles and I will go to his execution—to be witnesses to his death. He must not die alone."

Sarah swallowed. "I will go, too, Papa."

"No, Sarah. It is not easy to see a man die."

"I know," she said, her voice barely a whisper. "But he is my friend! If he sees me, he will know I have not forgotten him."

"Yes," said Mrs. Poyntz, tears running down her face. "We must all be witnesses."

The day of the execution in early October dawned dull and gray. Already the southern gate outside the town of Vilvoorde was crowded with onlookers. Thomas Poyntz, his wife, Sarah, and Miles tried to get close to the circle of posts that acted as a fence in the middle of the clearing. In the center of the circle was a large pillar of wood.

Several lawyers and clergy entered the clearing and seated themselves. Then Sarah heard Miles gasp. "It's Master Tyndale."

The prisoner was led into the clearing. He was very thin, his clothes threadbare and dirty. But William Tyndale gazed steadily around the crowd of common people. His eyes seemed to light up as he recognized first one, then another. Then his eyes rested on the Poyntz family and Miles Walsh, and a smile flickered on his tired face.

"William Tyndale, we ask you one last time: will you recant your heresy?" boomed a loud voice from the direction of the seated men. Tyndale said nothing, but continued to gaze out over the crowd.

The prisoner's feet were then bound to the stake, and piles of brush and logs heaped around him. An iron chain was fastened around his neck, and a rope noose settled around his throat. "Praise God," Sarah heard her father murmur, "he will be strangled and not burned alive." Sarah squeezed her eyes shut, but they flew open when she heard Tyndale's clear, strong voice.

"Lord!" Master Tyndale cried. "Open the eyes of the King of England!"

Then the executioner came up behind the stake and pulled with all his strength on the noose. The crowd gasped as Tyndale's head fell limply to his chest. Sarah felt Miles's arm tighten around her waist, catching her as her knees buckled.

"Stand, Sarah," Miles whispered in her ear. "We must stand for his sake."

A lighted torch was touched to the brush and the flames leaped around Tyndale's lifeless body. Only when the chain was released and the charred form fell into the flames did Thomas Poyntz turn and lead his family out of the crowd.

In the carriage on the way back to Antwerp, Sarah's eyes burned with unshed tears. What had Master Tyndale prayed? *Open the eyes of the King of England!*

It was too late for that. William Tyndale was dead.

She, Sarah Poyntz, had failed.

Chapter 13

The Victory

SARAH AND MRS. POYNTZ did not tell Mrs. Gilly that Master Tyndale was dead. Each time they visited, the old woman gripped their hands and with great difficulty whispered his name. "Master T'dale?"

"He is in a better place," Sarah said, once again changing the old woman's bedding and combing her hair. "He regrets he cannot visit you."

Mrs. Gilly nodded and seemed satisfied.

But it seemed harder to visit the smelly rooms and sad families in the slums along the docks after Tyndale's death. ". . . as you have done it for the poorest of my brothers," Sarah kept muttering to herself as she hauled water or held a squalling infant for a sick mother, "you have done it for Me."

She would have quit if it weren't for her mother. Mrs. Poyntz was not a strong woman, but she somehow managed to keep the boarding house going, as well as prepare food and do sewing and mending for Mrs. Gilly and others. Sarah knew she had to keep going as long as her mother wasn't giving up.

Belgium's rainy winter set in a few months after William Tyndale's death. One day, during a downpour, Thomas Poyntz and Miles arrived home from a business trip to England. No sooner had they walked in the door than they dumped their wet cloaks on the floor of the entrance hall and herded Mrs. Poyntz and Sarah into the parlor, shutting the door behind them.

"Thomas! What is it?" cried Mrs. Poyntz.

Mr. Poyntz took a package from his pack and unwrapped it. "Here," he said, handing it to Sarah. It was a book with a leather cover.

Holding the book, Sarah read the engraved title: "The Holy Bible." She looked up. "What is it, Papa?"

"The complete Bible in English!" her father said, excitement in his voice. "Do you remember the manuscript you saved from Tyndale's room, Sarah? And how I took it away secretly, and wouldn't tell you what I had done with it? Well, I sent it to a notable scholar at Oxford who is sympathetic to Tyndale's work, a man named Coverdale. He used Tyndale's manuscripts and completed the translation."

Sarah opened the cover to the title page. She looked up in dismay. "But . . . it says, 'Translated by Miles Coverdale'! After all the work Master Tyndale did—all he suffered in prison!"

Miles nodded. "I know. I thought the same thing at first. But if Master Tyndale were here, he would say it is not his name that is important, only that the people can read the Scriptures for themselves."

"And besides," interrupted Mr. Poyntz, "if Tyndale's name were on this book, it would surely be rejected by the king. But as it is . . ." And Thomas Poyntz threw back his head and laughed.

"Thomas! What are you laughing about?" demanded his wife.

"Come, come," said Mr. Poyntz, drawing his wife and daughter to sit by the fire. Miles leaned against the mantle grinning.

"As you know, my dear, business has been poor lately, so we went to London trying to find new agents. But this time there were no searchers snooping around; we breezed right through customs. We didn't know what to make of it."

"Then Uncle Thomas decided to go to Oxford University to see this Coverdale," Miles interrupted. "To see if he had been able to do anything with Tyndale's manuscripts."

"But we were hardly prepared for what happened!" Mr. Poyntz said. "Coverdale received us warmly and placed this book—the whole Bible in English—into our hands. Then he told us that King Henry himself had been given a copy!"

"And King Henry said, . . ." Miles deepened his voice and held his head haughtily. "'Well, if there be no heresies in it, let it be spread abroad among all the people!'"

Sarah stared. "He said *what*?"

"He said, 'Let all the people read it!' You heard me, you goose."

"Thomas, I can hardly believe this," said Mrs. Poyntz. "King Henry has given his permission to publish the Scriptures in English?"

Sarah's thoughts were all in a jumble. What was it that Tyndale had prayed just before he died? *Lord, open the eyes of the King of England!*

"God answered Master Tyndale's prayer," she said in awe.

"That's right, Sarah," said her father gently. "Not only that, but who knows how God opened his eyes? Maybe the New Testament you gave to Queen Anne was part of what God used to break down the king's defenses."

"But then . . . why did God let Master Tyndale die? It was all for nothing!"

"I think not," said her father. "Don't you see? Tyndale has won! They could kill him, but they

113

couldn't kill his dream. Now every man, woman, and child in England can read God's Word for themselves—from the common plowboy to the king himself!"

"Then . . . Tyndale's work still goes on."

"And you helped make it happen." Miles gave Sarah a playful shove.

Sarah opened the Bible and gently turned its pages. "I never realized that God uses us to do His will—just like it says in the Lord's Prayer." She turned a few more pages and read . . .

"Thy kingdom come; Thy will be done,
In earth, as it is in heaven."

More About
William Tyndale

WILLIAM TYNDALE WAS BORN in the early 1490s near the Welsh border of England. Around the age of twenty, he went as a student to Magdalen College at Oxford, then on to Cambridge University. "Lutheran ideas" abounded at Cambridge in the early 1520s, so it is probable that Tyndale formed many of his Protestant convictions at this time.

Leaving the university in 1521, he joined the household of Sir John Walsh at Little Sodbury Manor in Gloucestershire county, apparently as a tutor to his two young sons; he may also have served as a chaplain for the Walsh household or as a secretary to Sir John.

The Walshes were well known for their hospitality to both nobility and clergy, and Tyndale engaged in many theological discussions around their table. He was shocked at the ignorance of Scripture displayed by the clerics, and to one he challenged, "If God grant me life, ere many years pass I will see that the boy behind the plow knows more of the Scriptures than thou dost!"

At that time the only English translation available was the hand-copied Wycliffe Bible (1380). Tyndale's passion grew to translate the Scriptures into the common language and have them printed mechanically, so that peasants and nobles alike could read God's Word for themselves. He accused the clergy of keeping the masses ignorant of what Scripture said to cover their own corruption and greed. For instance, selling "indulgences" (i.e., paying a fine to atone for one's sins) was making many clerics rich, and many had illegitimate "wives" and children.

It was not only his desire to translate the Bible that got Tyndale in trouble. He both preached and wrote that we are saved by faith alone, not by following the traditions of the Church; that God alone forgives sin and grants mercy; and that commoner and king alike are accountable only to God, not to the pope. He, along with other reformers, had many other so-called "heretical" ideas, including the belief that the elements of the Lord's Supper were not the physical presence of Jesus Christ, but symbols of His body and blood.

It was illegal at that time to translate the Scriptures into English without ecclesiastical approval, so Tyndale left Little Sodbury to seek permission for his project. He contacted Cuthbert Tunstall, the moderate bishop of London, but received no encouragement. So with the financial backing of people like Sir

John and Lady Anne Walsh and a wealthy cloth merchant named Humphrey Monmouth, Tyndale left England in 1524 to do his translation work in Europe.

In Hamburg, Germany, he worked on the New Testament, translating directly from the Greek and Hebrew texts. A printer in Cologne agreed to do the printing. However, word leaked out and opponents of the Reformation raided the print shop. But Tyndale had been warned and fled just in time with the pages that had come off the press thus far. One copy of this incomplete edition (1525) survives today.

A year later in 1526, the first complete New Testament was printed in Worms, Germany, a more reform-minded city. As copies were smuggled into England, the bishops themselves bought up hundreds of the books and had them burned—not realizing that the money went directly back to Tyndale and financed printing even more copies!

By 1530 Tyndale completed translating the first five books of the Old Testament from the Hebrew, along with writing several treatises such as, *The Parable of the Wicked Mammon*, and *The Obedience of a Christian Man*. In *Parable* he argued that justification is by faith alone; in *Obedience* he stated that Christians should obey the king and other civil authorities, unless that obedience came in conflict with God's Word.

A copy of *Obedience* was given to Anne Boleyn, a French-educated lady-in-waiting who became Queen in 1533. She in turn showed it to King Henry VIII, who loved it and proclaimed, "This book is for me and all kings to read!" King Henry, who was at odds with the pope over Henry's efforts to divorce his first wife, Catherine of Aragon, thought Tyndale would be a good scholar to write the king's propaganda. He sent an invitation to Tyndale, by a man named Steven Vaughn, saying he would be given safe passage and a salary if he would come to court.

Tyndale firmly refused. In fact, in *The Practice of Prelates*, he asserted that divorce was against God's will and King Henry should stick with his wife! This set the king against Tyndale, much to the satisfaction of the bishops who continued to see the reform-minded scholar as a troublemaker. The king proceeded to "solve" his problem of how to divorce Catherine through the Act of Supremacy, declaring himself head of the Church of England, even above the pope.

Anne Boleyn also came into possession of a copy of the English New Testament translated by Tyndale, and showed it to the king. (According to the Newberry Library in Chicago, Illinois, the 1534 edition of the Tyndale New Testament, printed in Antwerp, Belgium, was 81mm x 128mm or about 3¼" x 5".) Henry, however, denounced it, saying there was no need for an English Bible "at present," and if and when it was done, should be done by respected scholars within the Church, not a renegade priest who had skipped the country.

The hunt for William Tyndale by English authorities intensified. But in 1534, Thomas Poyntz, an English merchant who was residing in Antwerp, Belgium, invited Tyndale into the protection of the English Merchants boarding house. (Poyntz, who was a relative of Lady Anne Walsh, eventually suffered much for befriending Tyndale; Humphrey Monmouth was also brought to trial and imprisoned for assisting "the heretic.")

In the spring of 1535, a university student named Henry Phillips made the acquaintance of the English merchants in Antwerp and eventually met William Tyndale himself. Tyndale was attracted to the young student's charming manner and seeming interest in reform ideas, though Thomas Poyntz was uneasy. His opinion was that Phillips "rings as false as a counterfeit coin."

Thomas Poyntz's distrust was justified. On May 21, 1535, Phillips showed up at the Poyntz home in Antwerp and invited Tyndale for lunch. As the two men walked through a narrow alleyway, soldiers captured Tyndale and hauled him off to Vilvoorde Prison. Poyntz's many efforts on Tyndale's behalf went unrewarded. In August 1536 Tyndale was tried and condemned as a heretic. In October of that same year, he was strangled and burnt at the stake.

Who used Henry Phillips, son of a notable English family who had fallen into disgrace for his gambling debts? It may have been Bishop Stokesley, the bishop of London after Cuthbert Tunstall and a fierce enemy of Protestantism. However, Phillips gained nothing from his betrayal of Tyndale; he himself had to flee from King Henry's agents and wrote letters home begging for his parents' help and forgiveness, bewailing his poverty and misery.

However, even while Tyndale sat in prison, a fellow Oxford scholar, Miles Coverdale, completed an English translation of the Bible, largely based on Tyndale's work. Only months after William Tyndale's death, King Henry put his stamp of approval on the Bible, and by 1539 every parish church was required to make copies available to its people.

For Further Reading

Christian History, Vol. VI, No. 4, Issue 16. This entire issue is devoted to William Tyndale. Available through Christianity Today Inc., 465 Gundersen Drive, Carol Stream, IL 60188.

Duffield, George, ed., *The Works of William Tyndale*, The Courtenay Library of Reformation Classics (Berkshire: The Sutton Courtenay Press, 1964).

Edwards, Brian H., *God's Outlaw* (Phillipsburg, N.J.: Evangelical Press, 1976, reprint, 1986).

"God's Outlaw: The Story of William Tyndale" (film/video), Gateway Films, Box 540, Worcester, PA 19490.

Walter, Henry, ed., *The Works of William Tyndale*, Parker Society Series (Cambridge: University Press, 1848-50; reprint London: Johnson Reprint Corp., 1968).